RANSOM

Shadow of an Empire

~

Book I

~

Cross of Secrets

By Thérèse Judeana

~

illustrated by Grace Bourget

En Route Books and Media, LLC
Saint Louis, MO

En Route Books and Media, LLC

5705 Rhodes Avenue

St. Louis, MO 63109

Contact us at contact@enroutebooksandmedia.com

Cover Credit: Grace Bourget

ISBN-13: 979-8-88870-026-6 and 979-8-88870-030-3

Library of Congress Control Number: 2023930334

Acknowledgments

The author would like to thank her friends and acquaintances who made suggestions and gave advice; thanks to Chantal LaFortune for feedback and her enthusiasm in reading it.

Most of all, thanks to Christ the True Ransomer for rescuing us all, in time, eternity, and every day of our lives.

Dedication

O Lord I offer Thee This work through Thy only Son,
in the power of the Holy Spirit,
to the praise of Thy eternal Majesty.

- St. Gertrude the Great

To the Hearts of the Holy Family.
In honor of the Holy Face of Christ and Our Lady of La Salette,
that it might help to dry their tears.
For all those who are searching for the key to freedom from sin and
hope in this vale of tears.
And to my Ransomer and my Daystar.

Book I

Cross of Secrets

RANSOM

Book I: Cross of Secrets

~~~

"Consider what is the price given for your ransom, and you will never more be slave to any man on earth. This reward and ransom is the Cross. . . . you should impress it on your heart with the love of a fervent faith."

– St. John Chrysostom, On the Mystery of the Cross

I

Silence

The star cruiser glided slowly through the starry void, its engines humming softly as they glowed a gentle blue. A shimmering wave of cosmic dust scattered slowly through the vacuum of space, tossed out by a centuries' dead star.

The captain paced his quarters, glancing out of the panoramic viewports every now and then. There seemed nothing to hold back the airless vacuum of death. Nothing but a thin sheet of glass – plasma treated, yes, but thin nonetheless. Not even a faint flicker of a reflection gave away the fact that it protected him. The silver hull of the ship seemed to drop away below him as he stood there, a lone eagle perched on a sail-less mast of its master's ship.

The captain sighed. Some might find deep space beautiful; he only saw its loneliness. Its coldness. Its death.

A soft beep echoed through the cabin. The captain turned and glanced at the computer console nearby. It was an alarm, reminding him that in a little under an hour the *Lumenara V* would rendezvous with the *Delta IV*. The *Delta* was a missionary cruiser, under commission from the Order of the Savior's Ransom, a group which raised money to save those unfortunate souls caught in slavery throughout the galaxy of Andromeda, and, when necessary, fought for their freedom.

It was Captain Marc Hesslin's orders to rendezvous with the *Delta* so that the rescued prisoners might be transported to their respective homeworlds. Marc gazed out at the stars again and felt another chill run through him. The only respite from this coldness was the act of mercy which he was performing. Such work saved his embittered soul from sinking into its despair again. It kept his restless heart busy, and crowded out unwanted thoughts.

He sighed and activated the comlink. "Lieutenant Briggs, how long until we dock with the *Delta IV*?"

"Approximately 45 minutes and 25 seconds, sir," Briggs' voice crackled over the intercom. Marc made a mental note to have the engineers correct the transmitter in his cabin.

"Thank you, Lieutenant." He signed off. He beat his hands restlessly on the desk for a moment. He needed to busy himself. He strode to the doorway and waved his hand over the activation sensor. The door slid soundlessly open and he exited.

Making his way through the brightly lit corridors, Marc had to marvel once again at the artificial sunlight which beamed through every other window. How confusing it was, though, to pass one sunlit window only to pass another filled with the all-too real view of deep space!

Marc shook his head. The last ship he had commandeered had been much simpler and much more realistic. However, he was almost grateful for this attempt to cheer up the chill of space voyage. It would never help as much as the indoor common area, which boasted beautiful gardens with an intricate irrigation system, a grand library, stores, cafes, and even a playground for little ones.

Marc glanced over the balustrade. The entire center of the ship was hollow like one of those old-fashioned hotels people used to stay in, Marc remembered. Now such places were less of a mildly intriguing, relaxing getaway from life, than a luxurious, stampeding shock that ranged from bubble pods suspended several thousand feet above the earth to orbiting retreats.

With walls of concentric rings which made up the various balconnaded floors of the ship, the *Lumenara's* plaza offered everyone a refreshing view of something other than space and false sunlight.

Far below, Marc could see several of his commanding officers enjoying their morning coffee and even a doughnut which came close to those from bakeries back home. Marc found himself smiling as his eyes followed the officers' children, who ran about playing hide-and-seek in the garden bushes and splashing in the many fountains, shrieking with laughter all the while.

Oh, for the days when he could be so carefree! But they were over, Marc reminded himself, and nothing could bring them back. His only joy now would be to ensure that such days could continue for those in his care.

Feeling refreshed, Marc continued on and came to the elevator. He found the efficient young engineer, Samantha Anselle, waiting as well, busily tapping away on her tablet. She specialized in computers, but was the dependable kind who could be found wherever something went wrong with the ship's tech, as was all too frequent. The girl glanced up and hastily saluted him, nearly dropping her tech-bag.

"At ease!" the captain said, smiling. "Did I startle you, Ms. Anselle?"

"Just a little, sir," she admitted.

"How's the work on the new cooling system coming?"

"To be truthful, sir, we're having some trouble with the liquid coolant. It keeps freezing into a solid block. Which means it doesn't help cool anything because it won't pass through the system."

Marc gave her such a confused look that Samantha couldn't help but laugh. "If you care to come down later, sir, I'll show it to you if we haven't fixed it yet."

Marc figured that was a good idea. There was a soft whir as the hydraulic elevator reached their floor. They both stepped on.

"Floor?" asked Marc.

"Tech Center," Samantha replied. The Tech Center on Level 0 held all the ship's central computer servers, engines, heating and cooling systems, and was where most electrical equipment was stationed.

"I guess that was obvious," the Captain remarked. He ordered the computer to stop the elevators at Levels 5 and 0.

The hydraulics whirred softly for a moment, and then the elevator descended swiftly and smoothly, flashing past floor after floor. There was a gentle bump, a moment's pause, and the doors slid open to show the plaza full of laughing, chattering officers and their families. The scent of freshly baked goods wafted over the sounds of the dancing fountains.

Marc took in a deep breath, smiling as he looked out. This was where he felt best – and yet at his worst because he alone *was* alone. He stepped out, bidding good day to Samantha, who moved to the edge of the elevator. Stopping the door by laying her hand upon it, she looked out with a wondering smile. She sighed softly.

"I don't get to spend much time up here," she breathed. "It's so . . . homey. Cheerful. No whirring of the engines, panicky coolants, fused wires . . . no burning heat from the energy cells. And there's that sunlight–"

She tipped back her head to look at the domed ceiling of the ship, high above. Clouds softly waved across an azure sky, and a fan-generated breeze gently blew through the terraced gardens.

"This has to be the most wonderful ship in the fleet," she murmured. ". . . Except for the Tech Center." She made a face. "At least I know how to function there. Up here . . . it's awkward. Like I'm a spider out of its web." She sighed again and stepped back into the elevator.

Marc was staring at her.

"Wait." He stopped the door. "You said you hardly get to be up here?"

Samantha looked at him, nonplussed. "Oh, it's normal," she explained. "That's how it works. I'm an engineer-on-call. I'm not allowed to leave the Tech Center unless called for. I had to fix a computer for Major Haynes; otherwise, I'd have spent all day down there."

Marc's eyebrows arched. His expression as he pictured spending a day in the white-walled halls and corridors of the Tech Center, packed with noisy computers, whirring hydraulics, and flickering lights, must have been amusing. Samantha laughed and assured him that the situation was quite alright. She bid him good day once more.

"Wait!" he insisted. He leaned into the elevator, ignoring the incessant calling for the elevator from Level 19. He opened the comlink.

"Hesslin to IT." After a brief silence, Chief Engineer Truitt Yarborough answered.

"Truitt here, Captain."

"Truitt, can the computer emergencies be managed without Ms. Anselle today?"

"Well, I suppose so, Sir. Young Konstan can take her place."

"Thank you, Truitt. Out."

Turning, Marc found Samantha staring at him with huge emerald eyes. He shrugged.

"What?"

"You . . . asked for me to take the day off. I've never had a day off, sir." She studied his face with wondering, grateful eyes. "Thank you!"

Marc smiled, just relieved to have taken his mind off himself. "That's quite alright, Ms. Anselle. I'll show you around."

"Thank you, sir," Samantha said respectfully. She demurely glanced up at the insistently flashing call light placed above the elevator's control panel. "I think we should let the callers on Level 19 have their elevator," she suggested.

Marc motioned for the computer to disregard the order for Level 0 and the pair stepped off. They watched the elevator zoom up to meet the anxiously waiting would-be passengers.

Samantha looked around. The green of the gardens, the crystal water of the fountains, the golden light from above, the happy children and loving parents – her eyes closed as the breeze kissed her face.

"It reminds me of home," she breathed. She opened her eyes. "Back on Almedra . . . before the meteor struck."

A tremor and a shadow passed over her face. Soon the customary light returned to her eyes as she steadied herself. "That was a terrible time. I'm grateful to be here, even if it means that I'm stuck in a Tech

Center ninety-nine percent of my life." She glanced at Marc, who was watching her with a grave respect.

"It's why I look forward to every rendezvous with a mission ship like the *Delta IV*," she said. "The *Triad* rescued my people. The Almedrans used to be a favorite target of the slave trade; consequently, there's always a ship of the Order on patrol in our system. Most of us died with the planet, but those who were left found new lives, new homes, new jobs, and hopeful futures because of the Order of the Savior's Ransom." She turned to look again over the plaza.

"Because of them we have a chance to help others. Without them . . ." she looked at Marc. "My people would have been destroyed, just as many others have been through natural and unnatural disasters, like slavery."

Marc murmured a quiet note of sympathy. His mind flashed briefly to his own past with the Order, but he blocked it. There was no need to reflect upon what he had already lived, he told himself. Every fiber of his being already knew what he had been through.

"How long until the rendezvous?" Samantha asked, turning to him. Marc glanced at his watch.

"Thirty minutes, or thereabouts," he answered. They began to stroll across the plaza, dodging rogue balls that rolled away from the children.

"How old were you when it happened?" Marc glanced at her. "Almedra, I mean."

"I was eight years old," Samantha admitted. "I was the youngest in my family. I remember being terrified -"

Her gaze wandered about the plaza as if she could see the flaming meteors once more.

"It was glowing red and orange everywhere I looked . . . there was so much pain . . . screams and weeping. If the *Triad* hadn't been in the system, we all would have perished."

"And after?" Marc prompted her.

"Afterward my family and I were taken to Danya, in the system of A'cile. My father found work as a jeweler, but my grandparents needed to be supported as well. I started working in a tech shop and eventually made my way to the Academy of Engineering. And from there," she shrugged, "to here." She looked askance at him.

"And you, Captain? If you don't mind my asking."

Marc felt every muscle in his body grow taut. He exhaled. "I'm sorry, Ms. Anselle. I don't like to speak of my past. I'm still attempting to process it. There are only a few who know what happened." He felt it necessary to apologize. "I'm sorry. It's not fair for me to ask about your difficult past and then not explain my own. Perhaps someday I can right that." He met her gaze and found it to be sympathetic.

"No," Samantha said quietly. "There's nothing to right, Captain. I told you freely of my past, and I would never ask anyone to tell me of their own if it were not told with a similar freedom. If it hurts you, I do not ask it of you."

Marc smiled gratefully at her. At that moment there was a soft musical ding over the ship's communications systems.

"Twenty-five minutes to rendezvous with *Delta IV*, twenty-five minutes to rendezvous. Captain to bridge, please, Captain to bridge."

Marc looked up. "Well, there goes our tour," he said regretfully. "Perhaps another time, Ms. Anselle."

"That's alright, sir," Samantha quickly assured him. "If you don't mind, sir, since it's my day off . . . I'd like to be on hand when we dock with *Delta IV*. Just in case there's anything that needs doing." Marc gladly gave her his permission.

"Back to the elevators!" Samantha laughed, and they boarded again. It zipped swiftly up to Level 21.

The doors slid open upon the bridge, with its sophisticated computers, softly blinking lights in starlit hues, silver plating, and the huge panoramic windows revealing thousands of stars and solar systems. Samantha caught her breath and gazed out into the expanse.

"It's been a long time since I saw so many stars," she whispered. She navigated her way around Hulls, the ship's weapons officer, Vidara the communications officer, and Lieutenant Commander Briggs. She stood before the window, gazing out with delight as the *Delta IV* came slowly into view.

Just a silvery glistening dot with a faint tinge of blue, the ship came on steadily until they could see the yellow glow of the windows on its many decks, and even the command center. It was a large ship, nearly equal in size to the *Lumenara,* and was capable of carrying several thousand passengers.

"Isn't she a beautiful ship?" Samantha breathed. Marc was standing beside her. He gave her a sideways look.

"Haven't you seen <u>our</u> ship from the outside?"

The young woman smiled in amusement. "Only a few times, sir."

"I should have known." Shaking his head, Marc took his seat as the *Delta IV* hailed them.

"This is Captain Aldo Berron of *Delta IV*. *Lumenara V*, we have you in sight."

Marc answered the hail. "This is Captain Marc Hesslin of *Lumenara V*. *Delta IV*, it's a joy to see you!"

"Thank you, *Lumenara*; estimated docking time will be in approximately seventeen minutes."

"Begin docking procedures," Marc ordered his crew. He turned back to watch the approaching ship. "*Delta IV*, you've no idea how glad I am to see you!" he murmured.

~~~

Captain Aldo Berron turned to his aide, Senior Officer Anthony McGuirk. "Captain Marc Hesslin! Not the Marc Hesslin of the Battle of Maltara?"

McGuirk nodded. "The same, sir. If not for him, slave traders would have captured and destroyed every people in the entire twenty-three-planet system. He doesn't care to be known as a war hero, though."

"But I heard that he disappeared fifteen years ago!"

"He did, sir; but two years ago, he was found adrift in the time-warp fields of Borania. Apparently, his ship had been attacked in one time or another."

Berron frowned. "Any idea what happened to him during those thirteen years?"

"He didn't have good luck, sir . . . according to rumor he married the most beautiful woman in the constellation of Cygnus, a Cythian, and had a child. It seems something happened to both mother and child, and he went searching for them. But it's also quite possible that he was simply lost in a time warp. Records state that he won't speak of those thirteen years, sir."

Berron turned back to the viewports. "Marc Hesslin, savior of a solar system . . . what has life done to you?" he muttered.

II

Refuge

There was a muffled *clunk* as the docking ports met and locked. A hiss of oxygen followed with a whir of hydraulics, and the steel-plated doors slid seamlessly open before Marc Hesslin. Before him stood Captain Berron, Senior Officer McGuirk, and a tall, metal and starcloth-clad officer, Robert Ransomme of the Order of the Savior's Ransom. The coat of arms was emblazoned upon his uniform, and his cloak and pauldrons indicated his rank as a senior knight.

"Captain Hesslin!" Berron stepped forward and clasped his hand. "It's an honor to meet you, sir. I was a lieutenant in the Battle of Maltara," he explained.

"Captain Berron! Mere actions do not create an aura of heroism," Marc answered dryly. "But you, at least, understand what it meant to be in the battle." He turned and Berron introduced McGuirk and the mysterious, bearded Ransomme.

The knight stepped forward. His eyes were hooded but glowed with the light of his zeal for his work.

"Captain Hesslin," he said. "Perhaps it seems of little honor in your eyes, but your actions saved a system from the slavery the Order strives to end. It is a pleasure for me to meet you, Captain." He extended his hand to the discomfited Marc.

"Your actions at Maltara deserved for you the cross of the Order which you have borne ever since." Marc started, wondering if the knight could possibly know that he was still wearing the crimson enamel cross beneath his uniform.

"Lord Ransomme," he answered respectfully but a trifle stiffly, "you are the one who deserves the praise. You have dedicated your entire life to saving souls from worldly chains. I simply did my duty."

"You did what was right," Ransomme replied, "because you knew it to be so. But come," he declared, noting that Marc was eager to close the topic. "We have two thousand of those poor souls aboard the *Delta IV*. We have received a distress call from the system of Alterra, and we must make haste. As soon as our refugees have been safely transferred and have received rooms and the required medical exam, we must depart."

"I understand," Marc replied. "Shall we begin?"

The other three nodded. The next few hours were a constant stream of grateful refugees, men, women, and children from all systems. Files were filled out, medical exams were made, rooms were assigned, and sympathies and encouraging words were passed out.

"Pell, see to it that each refugee receives new clothing, as well," Marc ordered his first officer.

"Yes, sir!" Pell replied, and sent out a notice that clothing was to be made for each individual.

"Captain!"

Marc turned and found Samantha struggling through the crowd.

"Sir!" she said. "Permission to join the volunteer transferal crew?" Marc gave it rather distractedly. Samantha rushed off.

At last, the first five hundred refugees were through and situated, and there was a brief lull as the next five hundred had their files filled out. These files contained personal information such as name, age, home-world, occupation, talents, and so forth, to help get them all organized.

"Captain Hesslin." Marc turned again and found Lord Ransomme at his side. "While we wait for our jobs to resume, let us take advantage of God's gift of rest." Ransomme invited Marc to walk with him. Strolling through the corridors, Marc could not help but remark that the knight's name was rather unusual.

"As a Knight of the Order of the Savior's Ransom, we all take a similar name," Ransomme replied. "The surname 'Robert' becomes one of our own, a symbol of the attempted robbery of life and soul by the act of slavery, while 'Ransomme' is given to us to remind us of our mission. To avoid confusion we're generally known by our middle name, which remains our own. Now, in my case, I was born 'Robert,' therefore I had no need to take the name. I am actually the only real 'Robert Ransomme' in the entire Order of seventeen hundred knights."

There was silence for a moment as the pair stepped out onto Level 5. Approaching the balustrade, they looked out over the plaza. Teaming with happy families more than ever, it was a beautiful sight.

"Those poor souls," murmured Ransomme. "Many of them have never known any home other than a dark, dank pit. No food but scraps and what bits of pitiful life they can consume." He turned to Marc and studied him with the keen eyes of an eagle.

"Captain," he said very slowly, "I heard a curious thing from my superior, General Richards. I wonder . . . . perhaps you could enlighten me."

"I would be glad to if I may," Marc responded, turning to face the knight. Ransomme gazed out over the plaza.

"I heard tale of a man whose wife and child – a daughter, I believe – were taken by a troop of Marauders, and quite possibly sold into slavery. Now, apparently," he said, "the father escaped and called in my Order for help, but no trace of the captives could be found."

Marc went very still. His eyes traced the mosaic pattern of the plaza floor below over and over.

"The same man was found years later, drifting in the time-warp fields of Borania," Ransomme continued. His eyes fastened on Marc's face, like a cat's eyes upon a sparrow. There was a moment's silence. "You know of whom I speak, Marc."

Marc turned sharply away. A rattling breath drew through his lungs as he struck his hands upon the balustrade.

"I know it hurts you, Marc," Ransomme said softly. "If you don't face and accept your past, it will haunt you forever. Your wife and daughter would not wish this for you."

"And I never wanted slavery for them!" Marc hissed through gritted teeth. "Yet it was my idiocy which led to their pain and mine!"

Ransomme looked at him seriously. "What idiocy?"

"I was called to meet with other commanders of the Vestar Fleet," Marc muttered. "I was an idiot to not realize that it was a false call! It was the Marauders' wish to remove me from the planet Cytha because they were afraid I could defeat them . . . without my ship! That's what heroism did for me!" He turned his head away. Another silence.

"Do you believe them to be alive?"

Marc struck the railing again and forced himself to shake his head no. He turned to Ransomme with a haunted look.

"The ship took them through a time-warp," he whispered. "I followed them through the fields of Borania; they caught me in their tractor beam and brought me onboard, but when I tried to escape with my family, the Marauders threw me out into the fields. I tried to follow the ship, but lost them in endless time rifts." He turned away again.

"It was in one of those time-warps that I called upon the Order," he confessed. "They did everything they could, but I didn't realize that it was five years after the fact. Then I warped again and again, dying a little more each time. I couldn't escape the fields, and I couldn't find my Talitha and my little daughter -" he hung his head.

"Finally, the Order found me floating out there and brought me back." He looked out over the plaza in misery. "If the Marauders alone can navigate those fields without being lost in time. . . I'll never know where they went! Worse yet, they matched the description of an ancient tribe from a thousand years ago. They were time-travelers. Likely my darlings died a millenia ago!"

Ransomme watched him. He gently laid his hand on his shoulder.

"This is why you protect refugees, then," he said softly. "This is why you bury yourself in work. May God bless you and have mercy on you, Marc! . . . Come. Work will do you a world of good."

Marc straightened in his agony and followed the knight back to the docking station. . . back to work. Back to try and prevent the same thing which had happened to his family, from happening to these refugees. Back to a life-long living death. Again.

III

Echo

Samantha picked up the lost youngster who had nearly been trampled on in the crowded transfer area. "It's alright!" she soothed the tearful child. "Let's find your mother." Shifting the child to her hip, she called out, "Whose child is this?"

A woman swiftly pressed her way through the noisy throng and took the child away with a grateful smile. Samantha smiled back and watched as the mother disappeared again. The young woman looked around. A constant but slow stream of refugees lined up, were given their transfer files, and guided through the doors and into the *Lumenara V*. Almost every refugee wore only rags and scars.

Samantha whispered a prayer for them all as she hastily joined the rest of the volunteers in attempting to alphabetically organize the group. Soon after someone called for an engineer to fix a statically operating computer.

Opening her emergency tool kit which she always wore clipped to her belt, Samantha pried open the front panel and peered inside. Within five minutes, she had rerouted several finicky electrical currents and slammed the panel shut. The computer screen came back up with a happy beep and Samantha found herself being dragged off to fix one of the precious 3d-printers which was spouting out a hundred copies of the same ID tag.

At last, Samantha collapsed against a wall and noticed, after a moment's respite, that there were only a few straggling refugees left.

She blew a loose lock of hair out of her face. Her feet ached, her eyes ached, and her heart ached. She looked around.

Her eyes stopped on a young girl who was standing off by herself, gazing at one of the many flickering panels of false moonlight. The maid's back was to Samantha, but it was clear that the girl was not looking forward to the transfer. Samantha felt a twinge of sympathy and made her way over to the girl.

"Hey," she said softly. "You're the last one. Aren't you looking forward to going home?"

The girl turned to look at her. She seemed to be about fifteen years of age, but her eyes were solemn with the clear wisdom that comes with suffering.

"I cannot go home," she answered in a delicately musical voice. "There is no home for me to go to anymore."

"I'm sorry," Samantha murmured. "I literally lost my home too, when I was young. There was a meteor shower which destroyed the planet." She exhaled and gave the girl a smile. "What's your name?"

The girl shook her head. "I lost my family," she murmured. "I promised myself that no one would speak my name again. But you may call me . . . " she searched for a name. "Tristelle," she said finally. Samantha understood. She squeezed the girl's hand.

"Come on," she said. "I'll help you get through the transfer. I've been helping all day, so I know how it works."

The maid smiled quietly and accepted the offer. They made their way through the line, getting the files finalized and processed, found that there were no more available cabins, and were promptly told to meet Dr. Elise Menendez of the *Lumenara V* for the standard medical exam. Samantha led her companion to the *Lumenara's* infirmary, only to be gently pulled to a halt. She turned in surprise.

"Please," said the maid, "I do not wish to be examined. There is nothing wrong with me. I am neither ill, nor injured, and I feel alright."

Samantha felt a bit bewildered, but she understood.

"If it makes you uncomfortable, and you're certain that you're alright, I'll ask her to give you a pass," she replied. "But you'll still need to be screened for any hazardous bacteria." This Tristelle agreed to, and was relieved when the young, pretty doctor smiled and told her that all was well. The maid thanked her gratefully and followed Samantha out. A few minutes later they were standing in the plaza.

"Well," Samantha sighed, glancing around, "since the cabins are all full, I'll have you stay with me." She looked at the girl to see if that was alright. Tristelle nodded.

"I know you must be starving after all that," the engineer continued, "so before we get a new dress made for you, we'll grab something to eat."

She led the girl to a nearby bakery, where they both tried an unusual lingonberry and cream-cheese pastry and a fruit salad.

Then Samantha guided her new friend through the plaza, watching as the maid's eyes grew huge upon seeing the massive gardens with flowering vines and sparkling brooks.

"Why," she said softly, "this is like the gardens back home! Even the bricks are like the Cythian stones."

"I understand that our captain designed them himself," Samantha replied. "I heard him say that he had lived briefly on Cytha."

"Then there is a bit of home for me here," murmured the girl. Suddenly she brightened. "Is there a chapel onboard?"

Samantha nodded. "I'll take you there after we have dinner tonight," she told her. "But now, a dress."

She led the way to the onboard Academy of Design, where specially designed computers would visually take an individual's measurements and create any desired garment. Despite being a computer engineer and having fixed a few snags in the software, Samantha had never utilized this technology herself, so she simply had to experiment so that she could show her companion what to do.

She was rather amused when she realized that she had accidentally ordered a shawl instead of a scarf. She laughingly stuffed the shawl back into the machine, whereupon it was instantly recycled into another customer's coat. She raised her eyebrows at Tristelle, who smiled in reply and stepped onto the computer platform. In less than a minute she had been measured and was staring at five thousand garment options.

"I wish I had a Cythian dress like my mother used to wear," she said longingly. Instantaneously several Cythian styles popped up on the screen. The girl exclaimed softly in delight and quickly chose one. Samantha stared.

"How odd!" she exclaimed. "This computer isn't supposed to have voice commands. Maybe the software was just updated?"

They both shrugged and watched happily as, in mere minutes, a simple but beautiful Cythian dress was created before their eyes. This stop was followed by a quick shower in Samantha's cabin.

Samantha left her new roommate to herself for a time. Her mind was clicking very rapidly. Tristelle had lightly explained her story and

Samantha wanted to see the Captain. She headed to the briefing room and waited outside. She knew that Marc would be conversing with his senior officers as well as Captain Berron and Lord Ransomme.

She was staring thoughtfully at a familiar Cythian piece of artwork when the doors of the briefing room finally opened and Marc exited. He interrupted his conversation with Lieutenant Briggs when he saw Samantha.

"Waiting for us, Ms. Anselle?" he asked, pausing. Samantha turned and looked keenly at him.

"Yes. Permission to ask an odd question?"

"Permission granted."

The engineer's eyes flickered to the rest of the group. The officers noted it and quickly proceeded down the hall.

Samantha turned back to Marc and asked bluntly: "Have you ever been married?" Marc stared.

"That's . . . what I call an odd question. Yes. Once. A long time ago. Long as in fifteen years."

"Good! That's what I wondered." Samantha walked away. Marc stared after her and turned back to see the Cythian image of Our Lady of the Sunrise. He sighed and shrugged at her, wondering what was up with his engineer-on-call. He, too, walked away.

~~~

Samantha, humming to herself, headed down to check on the Tech Center. Everything seemed to be under control, even the finicky coolant. She made sure to thank Truitt and Konstan for allowing her to take the day off.

"That's quite alright," Truitt replied. "You've hardly seen the light of day since you joined the crew, Sahma." This was Samantha's nickname among her friends.

"That's true, Sahma. Even I've seen every deck on the *Lumenara V*, and I've been here two years less than you," Konstan reminded her. The generally mischievous assistant engineer, only seventeen, treated her as his sister, and thus his sky-blue eyes were unusually serious.

"By the way," Truitt interjected, "I heard that you have a refugee staying with you. You'll be interested to know that the Captain will be formally welcoming all the refugees at precisely –" he checked his watch. "Six p.m."

"That means I have less than two hours beforehand," Samantha calculated, "and I promised to show her the chapel after dinner. I'd better hurry! Thanks again!" She flew out of the Tech Center and hastened to her cabin on Level 1, where she found her quiet young roommate dressed in Cythian style, kneeling to pray. Samantha waited respectfully until the maid finished and looked up.

"Shall we eat now?" the girl inquired.

Samantha nodded, and explained about the Captain's welcome speech on the way to the plaza.

"We won't have much time in the chapel," she warned, "and right now I know that God would want you to eat well, and slowly! Or you'll hurt yourself if you rush."

Her companion accepted this. They sat down to eat a healthy meal of salad, fresh fruit, whole grain bread, and a few appetizers. The maid picked up a small round toast, broiled with a sharp, crispy cheese and rosemary-herb butter.

"I have eaten this before!" she said. "Back home, I think. What are they?"

"They're called crudiccis," Samantha answered, popping a slice of blackberry havarti into her mouth. "I think it's another thing which the Captain introduced. I'm sure you'll encounter plenty of Cythian food around here. He seems to really have loved living on Cytha."

"That is good for me," the maid murmured, smiling at the toast in her hand. "It is almost like being home." Samantha smiled, too, glad that her companion was warming to the *Lumenara V*.

"Speaking of the captain," she remarked, dunking a strawberry into her yogurt, "I'm looking forward to the welcome speech. Afterward there will be a chance for the refugees to speak with him. He could use a friend who understands loneliness." She looked across the table at the girl who sat contentedly eating only the spinach from her salad. A Cythian trait, perhaps. "With the common love of Cytha, I think it would be good for both of you."

Tristelle looked up and studied her friend's face. "I will meet him," she said softly, "if you think that it will help him."

Samantha nodded and they finished eating. It was now quarter to five, and the engineer was eventually coaxed into leading the way to the chapel. It was beautifully designed to look like a morning sunrise, the sun being the beautiful gold tabernacle, atop which the monstrance was constantly placed for adoration. The chapel was gilded, with soft hues of arctic blue, cream, and peach imitating a morning sky. Sunlit windows made the pair almost feel as if they were at their respective homes.

"But this *is* home," Tristelle whispered, gazing adoringly at the Host, "because this is Christ."

IV

Restored

Samantha breathlessly checked her watch as she darted down the corridor. She and her friend had been in the chapel for almost fifty minutes, and as the auditorium was a fifteen-minute walk away, they would likely miss the Captain's entire speech!

At least it's not mandatory, Samantha reminded herself as she slid to a stop at the auditorium door. It slipped open and the pair entered. The auditorium was packed with refugees.

Searching the crowd with her eyes, Samantha led Tristelle to the last two empty seats. As they sat down, Samantha realized that the Captain had only just mounted the stage; that was lucky, she thought, and sat back to listen.

"On behalf of the entire Vestar Fleet I welcome all of you to the *Lumenara V*," Marc's voice came clearly over the speakers. "I know how much you've all been through," he continued. "I know how much you've suffered. . . ." he paused, and evidently struggled with himself for a moment. Samantha noticed her companion striving to see over the rows and rows of refugees in front of her.

"I myself have been there," Marc said finally. "Not for long, but enough to know what it's like. Thanks to the work of the Order of the Savior's Ransom, all of us have been saved – but it would be more correct to say that we've been saved thanks to the Savior, Christ. Without Him, there wouldn't be any good people in this world, and no chance of freedom. With that in mind, let us all give a prayer of thanks to Christ, the True Ransomer."

A priest led the Our Father. There was a moment of silence and then Marc resumed his speech.

"For all those who have been taken from home, I pray that you will find a good future there; for those who have lost your homes, and have none to go to, I pray that you will find a new one with all the blessings of Christ. In the meantime, the *Lumenara V* was built to function as a welcoming place for all for as long as is necessary. If there is anything you need, you have only to ask."

Marc asked a question, but Samantha didn't hear it because her companion had finally caught sight of the speech-giver and had wrestled her way out into the aisle.

"A'da!" she cried. In the pause after the Captain's question, her cry echoed in the auditorium. Two thousand pairs of eyes looked to see who would interrupt the captain. Marc's eyes went wide and he whirled. He hadn't heard that name in years -

"A'da!"

Samantha struggled into the aisle to try and stop the girl. *Not now!* She was just in time to see the maid fly down the aisle and up to the stage. Tears streamed down the maid's cheeks as her shimmering, iridescent eyes gazed insistently into Marc's shocked face.

"*A'da!*"

"A-Aiyra?"

"A'da!" came the joyful repeat as the girl stretched out her arms through a rain of tears.

Marc fell to his knees at the stage edge and took the maid's face in his hands. Frantically he searched her eyes, so soft and unreal like her mother's.

"Aiyra?" She only nodded. "Aiyra! My baby girl!" Marc broke down and kissed his daughter's wet cheeks.

Samantha stood in the aisle as a smile formed on her lips. Her eyes met Konstan's and Truitt's; the engineers were completely bewildered. Samantha only shook her head and took her seat again. Her fellow engineers shrugged at each other and looked to the other officers who were present and equally astonished. They looked for someone else to explain it to them, but there was only the heart-torn father kneeling with his arms around his only child.

V

Memory

The doors opened and slid shut behind Samantha. She stood still a moment, standing in a shaft of starlight in the combined sunroom and conservatory. Marc arose from a Cythian garden bench and greeted her. Aiyra turned and smiled at Samantha. The engineer returned it then looked apprehensively at the captain.

"You asked for me, sir?"

"I did," he acknowledged. "Do you recall," he said, moving around the bench, "how I said I might right the discrepancy of knowledge between us?" Samantha dipped her head.

"I think it's best done now," Marc said quietly. He was smiling. "Or a lot of people on this ship are going to remain confused." He motioned for her to sit down on a second bench. She did so. Marc sat down and put his arms around Aiyra. He looked into his daughter's smiling eyes.

"Let's start from the beginning, Princess." He turned with a flickering smile back to the engineer.

"You may know," he said lightly, "that I was a supposed hero in the Battle of Maltara. But what no one likes to mention is that I was critically injured in said battle. Someone told me that there were healing waters on the planet of Cytha, so I decided to take his advice and made my way to the planet. Cytha, as is commonly known, is a planet of gardens, meadows, farmland, and seas. Having crash-landed due to my belief that I could still control a ship -" here he looked at his daughter who was laughing at him.

"I was discovered by a Cythian maiden, the most beautiful woman in all of the constellation of Cygnus, or even the entire world: and she wanted to take care of me." He looked down into Aiyra's eyes and smoothed her hair.

"You're going to look just like your mother," he murmured. Aiyra smiled and leaned her head on his shoulder. Samantha watched them both.

"Let me guess," she murmured. "You fell in love with the maiden and married her." Marc smiled a bit wryly.

"Some would say it was rash of me," he admitted. "I was only seventeen. Yet the same people wouldn't have questioned my role in the war," he muttered. Aiyra whispered tenderly to her father, bringing a smile back to his face. He turned back to Samantha.

"Yes," he answered her question, "I married Talitha. We were happy together. Less than a year later we had Aiyra –" he hugged his daughter – "And I thought that everything was well in my world."

A shadow flickered over his face as he gently touched his daughter's hair. There were a few moments of silence as Samantha waited patiently for him to continue.

Marc sighed. "One ordinarily happy day, when my little Aiyra was only a few years old, I received a call from the fleet for a reunion of all the commanders from the Battle of Maltara, in the same system."

"Pause, please!" Samantha interrupted. "Quick question: how did you wind up as a commander of a ship when you were only seventeen? I thought that the Galactic Alliance's specifications exclude anyone younger than twenty-one."

"They do," Marc replied. "It was only through a series of odd accidents that I became a Galactic Alliance commander." He explained that he had just finished his time at the Galactic Alliance academy a year before the battle occurred. At sixteen, he became a crew member aboard the *Sunstar*, one of the older battlecruisers. It had seen a dozen wars throughout the galaxy.

"It was a no-nonsense ship, and the same attitude was expected of the crew," Marc reminisced. "One had to be tough to serve aboard, and that was a quality I had to learn quickly." He had to put up with stern superiors, harsh orders, and detention if he failed in his duties.

The first "odd accident" occurred when a gaseous explosion in the control room when Marc happened to be carrying a message to the Chief Engineer. Because he was the only one standing in an open doorway, he was the only one who didn't pass out from inhaling the toxic gas.

Marc briefly explained that he had grabbed a gas mask and spent the next twenty-five minutes calling a safety-team to rescue the rest of the fallen crew, discovering how to contain the fumes, and filtering them out of the engine room.

Those actions moved him into the field of the security team, and led him to his second "odd accident." A few months into his new job, he joined a reconnaissance team sent to rescue the chief of security, Barto, who had been captured by a group of Maltaks, a group of space pirates. Without a doubt Barto was being used to find a way to take down the *Sunstar*.

"We spent twenty-four hours on the tropical moon of Yalar," Marc told Samantha. "It was steaming, and more than one of our crew fainted. Moreover, the forests were teaming with toxic and aggressive creatures, not a few of which we encountered."

Eventually only Marc and Lieutenant Ocura were left conscious. They finally discovered the Maltaks' base, a domed compound surrounded by laser cannons. These Marc found a way to disrupt the electrical components, thus rendering them useless for a time.

Once in the compound, though, Ocura was shot down and Marc was forced to sneak through the corridors alone. He located the security room and brought down the forcefields, releasing the locks on the prison compound as well. He managed to signal the *Sunstar* to fire upon the compound in five minutes, but realized that Barto was not with the rest of the prisoners.

The Maltaks were in the central tower of the compound, working on a disarming-beam which was focused upon the orbiting *Sunstar*. Barto was being forced to help break through the computers of the ship.

Marc ripped out the main electrical router and flung it in the center of the room. The wildly wriggling wires literally shocked and stunned the majority of the Maltaks, while he and Barto took out the rest. They smashed the disarming-beam with less than a minute to spare, and leapt out the tower window. They barely made it out of the compound before the *Sunstar* successfully blew it up.

"We took the shuttle back to the *Sunstar*," Marc sighed, "and when Barto told the Captain Martel everything that I had done, Martel turned to me and said, 'Son, from now on I want you at my side.' He made me a Lt. Commander Bar Five on the spot, Bar Five meaning the very highest in that position," he explained. "It meant that I served on the bridge, commanded every reconnaissance team, and received special training. And it's through that rank that I wound up as a commander."

Samantha stared. "Exactly . . . how?"

Marc laughed at the look on her face. "You're just like everyone else. You all seem to think that it's somehow amazing. It's not."

He told her that when a red alert came through, bringing the entire fleet to fight off the Marauders at Maltara, he had, of course, been on the *Sunstar*. It wasn't long into the battle that one of the Marauders' ships cloaked itself and blasted the bridge. The shields prevented the greatest damage, but there were plenty of casualties, including Captain Martel and his First Officer. With them both taken out of commission for the time being, only Marc could take the Captain's place.

"I had never imagined commanding a ship in my life," he admitted. "And I discovered that it was even harder than I had expected, especially on a battle-cruiser. . ."

With explosions occurring all over the ship, Marc stared out the viewports as he watched the fleet being decimated. A shock had been delivered by the Marauders' back-up of 200 cloaked battle ships. The fleet didn't stand a chance. Marc watched the flaming plasma of the wreckage being drawn in by the gravitational pull of the nearby planets. If the fleet lost, than every civilization on every one of the twenty-three planets would be enslaved.

"Father, help me!" he breathed involuntarily. He was too young to be in this. Taking a deep breath, he ordered the chief engineer to jury-rig the engines and the disabled weapons. There was only one chance to take.

He knew by the scans of the cloaked Marauder ships that they were the lightweight type-C battleships, only large enough for a few crewmen. Type-C ships could not rely on their fuel supply for more than a few hours, nor would the supply of energy for their plasma cannons remain constant. Thus, there had to be a sympathetic battle-station nearby, without which the Marauders would be at the fleet's mercy.

Marc ordered the ship to fire the hyperdrive while remaining stationary. The energy waves diffused by the engines would create a spatial field around any object, cloaked or uncloaked, for 1,000 miles. This field would be visible on the Sunstar's scanners. Hopefully it would lead them to the battle-station. Marc watched the continuous scans with anxious eyes. He ordered that the battle-shuttles be manned and deployed to take down as many of the detected ships as possible. He turned his eyes back to the scanner.

There! That huge spatial field! It was definitely a battle-station! He ordered the navigational officer to set the Sunstar in hyperdrive on a course directly for the battle-station.

"Long story short, we blew it up and the Marauders automatically lost," Marc finished. "Which leads me back to Cytha. Fast forward back to the last scene, Talitha encouraged me to go and meet with the other commanders. I finally agreed . . . promising to bring her and Aiyra each a gift."

"Unfortunately," he continued through gritted teeth, "it was only after I reached Maltara that I discovered that the whole thing was a ruse. I flew back to Cytha only to find that my worst fears were confirmed: Cytha was in ashes, and a Marauder ship was just leaving the planet. I followed them. I was captured when they activated their tractor beam, was briefly reunited with Talitha and Aiyra, only to be ejected into the time-warp fields of Borania for attempting to take control of the ship." Marc groaned a little bit.

"Ergo, I attempted to follow them but was promptly drawn into one warp after another. I wound up in a time five years after the fact, but without realizing that, begged the Order to help me find my family. They did their best . . . and discovered that the Marauders who attacked Cytha were an ancient band from thousand years ago, in our time expressly to replenish the slave trade. And it was hopeless to find my family."

"A'da," Aiyra gently intervened, "there is something you need to know. It is not an unusual fact that the ancient Marauders came to our time. I tried to tell Captain Berron, but he would not believe me. There is no such thing as a modern Marauder. They are an extinct race, yet they show up in every time period, continuing their 'trade' throughout time. That is why the slave trade cannot be broken . . . because it lives a thousand years ago and *every year since*. If they are threatened in one time, they only return home, where they cannot be followed. A'da, A'ma and I were taken back a thousand years!"

Marc stared at her. Aiyra turned to Samantha.

"Sahma," she said, "After A'ma and I were captured, we were sold, a thousand years ago, and taken forward a couple hundred years; to the now extinct civilization of the Boroks. Then we were sold again. After A'ma was killed I was sold time and time again, getting closer and closer to this year; at last I spent the last five years on Ela, an ancient jungle planet known for its stoneworks; the Order saved me there." Then, with a curious look, Aiyra turned back to her father.

"A'da," she said, "We were on a desert planet of the Maeli people. I worked in the deadly mines of radioactive crystal. They made A'ma stay home and wait for me every day. The king, Daruth, tried to make her marry him; she would not dishonor you, A'da, and he tried to put the crown on her. She refused to let it touch her, and he killed her." Her brow wrinkled.

"A'da," she said. "You found us! Don't you remember being there? You tried to save me and A'ma . . . remember?"

Marc obviously had no idea what she was speaking of. Aiyra's lips parted as she studied his eyes.

"A'da," she whispered, "you have to find us there. Or I died three hundred years ago!"

There was a shocked pause. "Aiyra, listen to me!" Marc soothed, grasping his daughter's shoulders. "Darling, you're here! You're *safe!* If something had happened to you three hundred years ago, you wouldn't be here," he reminded her. "Believe me, Aiyra."

"Then who saved me if it was not you, A'da?" she demanded, more than a little distressed.

"Are you sure it was me?"

"Yes. It was you, he looked like you and acted like you, and he knew only things that you would know: A'ma was convinced that it was you!" Aiyra insisted. "It is the only way I knew who you were, A'da, when I saw you on the stage. . ." she added.

Marc held her gaze a moment. His eyes flickered downwards as he struggled to remember if he had gone through everything she had described.

"Darling, I don't remember anything," he said finally. "It's possible that I went through a time warp which brought me to you and your mother, but is it possible that I could completely forget everything which happened?"

Aiyra frowned. She contemplated this for a moment. "If you had gone backwards in time," she answered slowly, "perhaps it could have wiped your memory. But I never knew what happened to you when you disappeared from Ahltarr. I suppose it is probable that the Ahltarr were onto your plans for saving A'ma and I, attacked you, and either purposely wiped your memory and sent you through time, or you simply hit your head and somehow wound up in another time warp."

Samantha, who had been sitting silently in the shadows, spoke up. "I've heard of certain individuals who, having passed through a rift in time, also had a time rift in their mind: both responsible for preventing them from forming memories of their time travels, and for sending them into different periods."

Marc, who had completely forgotten about Samantha, objected to the suggestion. "If that were true in my case, I wouldn't have any memories of the time spent in the fields of Borania; but I *do* have those memories. Is it possible that I could have forgotten just one?"

"'Time is a wave of shifting sand,'" Samantha quoted an old Galactic Alliance textbook. "The effects of time travel may vary between individuals. However, I think we have established that Aiyra is safe from the effects of what *could* have happened three hundred years ago." She arose to leave. "If you don't mind, sir, I have to go . . . back to the Tech Center."

Detecting a stiffness about her friend, Aiyra called after the engineer. She followed Samantha.

"Sahma, please stay." Samantha turned back when Marc also called her name. She looked at the captain. He must have known what was running through her mind. Marc knew that she was afraid others would think she was in love with him, with the abrupt shift in their relationship. In her mind, they would think badly of her.

"Samantha –" he hesitated to use her first name. "I wouldn't have called you here if I thought that anyone would think less of you for it; I won't let anyone say anything against you. It's not as if I can't have friends who are engineers. And you knew Aiyra was my daughter when you hardly knew anything about me. Is it wrong for me to be grateful? No one will misunderstand this, Samantha."

Somehow Samantha remained uncomforted. "Captain, I'm sure you would have somehow found her without me. But I understand, sir . . . even if no one else will." Samantha walked out, leaving Aiyra to convince her father that everything was alright.

~~~

Samantha dropped against the wall with a moan. Her heart was pounding painfully. She couldn't believe how poorly she had treated the Captain, just when he had become her friend!

Poor Marc! All he had wanted was to thank her, an outpouring of the joy of having his daughter safely beside him. And she had made him feel as if he had committed a crime! How could she retract it, explain that she hadn't intended to hurt him, but only to protect herself from fear? What if anyone had discovered her secret?

Somehow it hurt Samantha more for the Captain than for herself; but she dreaded that someone might have begun to watch them closely already. And now she couldn't face him! He had trusted her, more than anyone else! He had told her everything. . . . No one else knew the full story as he had given it to her. If only she could tell him everything that she had been through . . . ! Oh, if he would be the one she could trust!

Samantha passed a hand over her eyes, half hoping to find herself lying in bed the next morning. It didn't work. With another soft groan she got up and walked down the corridor to head to the Tech Center, her head bent in misery.

VI

Tremor

The *Lumenara V* glided silently through the starry void, the lights lining the silver hull flickering indigo and gold. It had been nearly three weeks since Marc and Aiyra had been reunited, and most of the refugees had been returned home. The ship was making its final trip, into the system of Galarouros to drop off a few remaining passengers at the ocean planet of Maedra.

Aiyra looked thoughtfully out into the deep black of space, crossed with streamers of faintly rainbow dust and gas of the nearby nebula. She was in her suite, which had been the cabin of First Officer Pell, but he had moved down the hall. Marc had transformed the room into a pretty bedroom for his daughter, and it was now connected to his own cabin which was just next to it.

The walls of her room were a soft white, and the room was lit by many dim lights of white and pale yellow like stars on the ceiling. Thick carpets were scattered across the floor, and a dais of sorts lifted one to the wide windows curtained by white silk draped with a print of willow leaves and butterflies. These curtains were, of course, more for a homey feel than for shutting out the light, as there was little to be had.

Beneath the window was a flat and deeply cushioned sofa, where Aiyra liked to sit and read one of the many books from the well-stocked shelves on the opposite wall. There was a harp in one corner, a tiered fountain with pools of floating lilies and candles in another, and flowering plants, ivies, and candles tucked into every corner, making the room look bejeweled.

Aiyra's bed and closet were separated into their own little room. The same spray of star-lights threaded across the ceiling, and a narrow shelf-like pool ran along the walls at waist height, again dotted with lilies and candles.

Aiyra's eyes slowly traversed her sitting room, noting how carefully Marc had designed it for comfort after those many years of slavery. Her gaze fell on an unbelievably tiny kitty snoring away in its nest of a furry blanket and she laughed. The kitten opened one eye, thumped its tail, rolled over, and was promptly asleep again.

Little Sage had been a gift from Marc when he had visited one of the drop-off planets. Aiyra hadn't been with him. She was still struggling to relearn, or rather, learn for the first time, to live in freedom. Civilization frightened her because she only knew those civilizations to which she had been enslaved.

Aiyra shuddered a bit and sat down beside her kitty, stroking Sage's soft fur. The past three weeks had been spent exploring the ship from top to bottom, except for the times when Marc was needed on the bridge, in a staff meeting, or when overseeing the refugees' departure from the *Lumenara*. Even then Aiyra had followed him around, for neither could yet bear to be parted, even for a few minutes.

Everything was an adventure for Aiyra: she had never known pretty, comfortable clothing, only rough rags for working in, nor beds or good food. She had never really heard music except a few raucous notes from casinos, and knew next to nothing about flowers and birds. In short, all she knew was pain, suffering, and work. Aiyra winced.

When her mother had been killed, Aiyra had been hustled into yet another transport, a cruiser crowded with slaves. For the first time in her life, she was alone. She had no support, no sympathy, and no love. That was the day she had learned to fend for herself; to bear trials and pain patiently; to be alone. But then, after five years of being strong, the Order of the Savior's Ransom had located the slave planet of Ela and had shut it down, saving her and her fellow captives.

Aiyra's eyes went thoughtfully to the little icon on the windowsill. Marc had saved it from their home on Cytha; it had been her mother's favorite. She stared fixedly at it for a moment. Now that she had been reunited with her father, in freedom, she had that support, sympathy, and love that she had needed all along. All the tears and the pain which she had bottled up all those years came out, and the hardness left. But not all the pain had come out into the light; perhaps she ought to tell him that –

"No, if I cannot even think about it, how can I talk about it?" she asked aloud, rubbing her forehead, and looking at Sage. The kitten opened one eye and blinked as if in agreement.

"Anyway, I hope A'da will be done soon. . ." she sighed, and swung her legs over the side of her couch. She was feeling lonely. Today was the one day that she was unable to be with her father. The captains and first officers of the Vestar Fleet ships were all in virtual meetings with the commander of the fleet. She thought she had heard something about the Marauders. As for Samantha, neither Marc nor

Aiyra had seen so much as the engineer's shadow in those three weeks.

A strange tingling pain pricked the nerves in Aiyra's neck and shoulders and ran through her arms, causing her to wince. The freezing sensation was a recurring one, and she wasn't sure what it was. She hadn't told Marc yet because she didn't want to worry him; he was so relieved to have her back she didn't want to spoil it by anything that turned out to be nothing.

Aiyra gently stroked Sage's little ears. The kitten opened one eye again and sleepily licked Aiyra's fingers before falling asleep again. A kitten who was perfectly content to be fast asleep wasn't the greatest of company at the moment.

Perhaps, Aiyra thought, she ought to take the chance to visit the infirmary just to see what this pain was. She looked at the door, undecided. While she was happy to explore the ship with her father, she wasn't sure about doing so on her own. But then again, there were only good people on this ship, she reasoned.

Aiyra went resolutely to the door. She poked her head out into the hallway and then shut the door softly behind her. Darting to the rail, she looked down into the nearly empty courtyard. She wondered if she should explore even more on her way to the infirmary. She decided against this plan, not knowing how soon Marc would be leaving the meeting. She didn't want him to catch her in the infirmary until she knew what was going on. She stepped into the elevator.

~~~

Meanwhile, Samantha was exiting another crowded elevator, on her way to fix a malfunctioning dryer on the laundry level (it kept spewing wet clothes onto the floor and tripping up their owners). The other passengers had been only too happy to let the engineer out, indeed, they had practically shoved her out – and Samantha found herself promptly pressed into service. Not for fixing the dryer, mind you: but to divide and conquer the mountain of soggy clothes it had vomited out, as the owners were apparently loath to do their wash a second time.

Thus began the first of several dozen tedious journeys from the immaculate line of dryers, with a length of glass panes behind (through which impatient clothing owners could view the cargo bay), across the wide white hall, dripping as she went, and to the massive yet claustrophobic washing room, which smelled of wet dog half the time.

"Ugh," Samantha groaned, lifting yet another mound of sopping wet clothing into her arms. "I'm an engineer, not a laundromat!" She glanced down at her now-drenched olive green and black uniform and sighed.

"Oh, well! When this is out of the way, at least I can get the real job done." She heaved the pile of clothing higher in her arms, and began the trek across the now slippery corridor. She had a hard time seeing where she was going, so in another instant, she collided with someone and wiped out, scattering the clothing across the floor.

"Samantha!" a voice exclaimed. She glanced up dazedly.

"Aiyra!" she said, laughing and wincing as she felt her wrist. She scrambled to her feet. "I'm sorry now that I didn't make that pile a little smaller," she remarked, and apologized for bumping into her friend.

"It is alright!" Aiyra said cheerfully. She began helping Samantha to gather up towels, uniforms, and aprons. Aiyra examined a jacket which was clearly not Samantha's. Looking up, she beheld the only half-leveled mountain and began to laugh.

"Oh, Samantha! Why were you pressed into service? Are they short on hands and long on engineers today?"

"No," Samantha replied, "I was supposed to fix the dryer that balked at all those loads of wash! Only, yes, nobody felt like picking it up. So here I am." Aiyra shook her head.

"I will help you," she offered with a smile. The engineer stopped and looked at her, her eyes softening. Aiyra read the look.

"It is alright. I do not mind work! . . . Not as long as it is free," she added. A tremor passed briefly over her face and then the light entered her eyes again. Samantha smiled.

"Well, if you want to." They delivered the clothing to a new washer and then returned to Mt. Laundry. They began dividing it up, but into manageable heaps this time. Aiyra pulled a boot from the pile. She looked at Samantha and they both laughed.

"Someone doesn't know the last thing about laundry," Samantha speculated.

"I guess not," Aiyra agreed. Within twenty minutes, the pair had completed their task.

"Victory!" Samantha proclaimed. "We came, we saw. . . .and we didn't *quite* conquer." Aiyra looked confused.

"Sorry, it's a reference to an ancient line from a few thousand years ago. Some soldier named Caesar, but he's not from my planet so I don't really know anything about him except that line. And his name," Samantha explained. She straightened and looked at the dryer.

"And now, onto the real task which should have been finished over an hour ago! Thank you for your help, Aiyra," she said briskly. "But aren't you keeping your father company today?"

"He is working right now. There is a virtual call from the commander of the Vestar Fleet, I think. At the moment, I am heading to the sick bay, as I have been having some – some – well, a tingling feeling in some of my nerves." Samantha frowned as she began to unscrew the plating on the dryer's computer panel.

"Didn't you tell your father?"

Aiyra shook her head. "I did not want to worry him. You see, I get rather strange allergies and illnesses sometimes," she explained. She watched as Samantha unplugged the dryer and began to shove it away from the wall. "That is probably all this is."

"Ouch!" came a sudden yelp, and Samantha jumped out from behind the dryer, cradling her wrist and shaking it out. There had been a piece of metal, apparently a lost war badge in with the laundry, which had pierced a weak point the inside of the machine, chopped some of the wires, and poked out of the back. Its latest offense had been to deliver a deep gash to the engineer's wrist, probably a parting shot from an overworked, and overloaded, dryer. Aiyra looked concerned.

"We might as well both go to the sick bay," she said sympathetically. "That gash is very deep."

"I guess you're right," Samantha sighed. "At least I know what's wrong with that thing, now. I'll ask Konstan to come up here with a better pair of gloves and a torch to melt the plating. When he's done that, I'll be able to fix the wiring and patch up the holes."

She flicked on her communications watch and called Konstan to deliver the message. Aiyra looked a bit confused, not knowing who the name belonged to. She figured she didn't need to know really, unless she happened to meet him. With a crew of nearly nine hundred and a capacity for carrying two thousand passengers, that wasn't all that likely. Samantha turned to her and smiled.

"Come on, let's get you to the doctor now." With that, the pair set off and were soon standing in the sick bay.

Dr. Menendez smiled at them, and Aiyra insisted that Samantha go first. A swift cleansing and the applying of an astringent, and the engineer was ready to return to duty. Samantha stopped in the lobby, though, and turned back, meaning to make sure that Aiyra was just having allergies. Aiyra took her place in the seat.

"How's your father today?" the doctor asked lightly, turning on a handheld medical scanner and running it over the girl's arm. Aiyra looked at the doctor, then at Samantha with a slightly annoyed expression and laughing eyes. It hadn't taken the girl more than two examinations to find out that the pretty doctor had an interest in the captain.

"He is fine . . . .just very, *very* busy with work," Aiyra answered seriously. The doctor looked almost imperceptibly disappointed.

"Well, I'm glad he has you back," she said. "He's always burying himself much too deeply in his work – hopefully he'll find he has more time for you now." As she spoke, she finished scanning Aiyra's arms and shoulders, and made as if to scan the girl's neck, where the pain seemed to be radiating from; but Aiyra gently lifted her hand and stopped her. Dr. Menendez looked at her.

"Pain in the nerves often generates from the spine," she said gently. "I've scanned the nerves which hurt, save the ones in your face and neck." Aiyra did not remove her hand. She looked disturbed. The doctor sighed. "Aiyra . . . As a doctor, I could order you to let me scan your head."

Aiyra flinched. "Can I come back later?" she asked tentatively.

Dr. Menendez sighed. "Very well. But speak to your father."

Aiyra did not answer, and hopped out of the chair. She saw Samantha's bewildered gaze and turned away, leaving without another word. Samantha hastily exited and followed the girl. She was already down the hall.

"Aiyra!" the engineer called. Aiyra stopped but didn't turn. "Aiyra, what is it?"

The girl sighed. Pivoting slowly, she met Samantha's eyes.

"It is a lot of things. You see," she whispered, "I have never been free before. I mean, I was just a few years of age when my mother and I were taken. I do not really know how to trust people, really, and I am afraid to tell A'da about the pain now. I do not want him to be hurt; he has hurt so much over me already." Samantha looked at her for a moment.

"Aiyra . . . sometimes, hiding things is not the route to take. A wound so big and so deep can't be hidden," she said softly. "It'll only widen as time passes. Love makes us hurt. Your father is here for you. That's *why* he's your father: to take care of you, to comfort you, to protect you, to *help* you." She hesitated. "And honestly, Aiyra, that's why I'm here, too. I'm going to help you, too, if I can." She searched Aiyra's now smiling eyes. "Alright?"

Aiyra nodded. "I am glad I was able to see you again, Sahma. I should go now; A'da might be looking for me." She squeezed the engineer's hand and darted off. Samantha looked after her and wondered.

VII

Home

Aiyra darted into her room just as Marc entered through the door that joined their cabins.

"Aiyra!" he exclaimed, and his daughter ran to him.

"A'da!" she whispered happily. Marc held her close for a moment. "A'da, what did he say?" Aiyra asked, looking up at him inquisitively. Marc smiled and shook his head.

"Nothing you need to know, sweetheart; just some information on the Marauders."

Aiyra studied him for a moment and considered telling him about the pain; but then she decided against it.

"Well, sweetie," Marc declared, "it's nearly lunchtime, and after that we'll have time to explore. I think we'll see the birds today." Aiyra stared at him wide-eyed.

"Birds?" she repeated. "You have birds? Why, A'da, you have *everything* on your ship, even birds!" He laughed.

"We have a lot of things. . . maybe not *everything*. But I do know we have lunch! Come on."

He led her out, and in a few minutes, they were grabbing green tea, fresh fruit, and a dish which some new, young, enthusiastic employee had created and named "space pasta." Contrary to the name, it wasn't an empty bowl, but its contents did seem rather . . . questionable. Aiyra examined the green substance with suspicion: apples, spinach, vanilla yogurt, and cheese don't mix, she thought;

but then she didn't really know what they were anyway, and was happy to find that it was enjoyable.

The next stop was the aviary, which, Marc explained, contained the various types of birds which were given as diplomatic gifts. The Vestar Fleet had decided that since it was based on Earth, it would regulate diplomatic gifts to be the most beautiful objects or creatures to be found there. Thus, each ship in each section of the fleet was specified to carry specific cargo; in this case, birds.

Marc swung open the steel door to the aviary to be greeted by a sometimes-cacophonous concert. Peacocks, swans, doves, birds of paradise, cockatoos, parrots, nightingales, larks, hawks, falcons, and warblers all mixed, singing and chattering. Aiyra put her hands to her head, laughing at the noise.

They were standing in a massive room, complete with mini habitats for the various bird species; waterfalls and brooks ran through forests and rocks, and wire walls partitioned off the different birds. Marc began teaching her about them.

"And this one is a cockatoo," he was saying, when a side-door swung open and a youth entered. Instantly the doves began cooing and the songbirds chirped when they saw him.

"Hullo," he laughed when one bluebird came and pulled inquisitively at the keys on his belt. A little white dove flew straight to his shoulder and nestled there. The boy smiled and gently stroked the dove's feathers.

"Hey, Konstan!" Marc said cheerfully as the young engineer spotted them. "What have you been up to lately?"

"Fixing a dryer most recently," the youth replied, advancing and stopping in front of them. The dove refused to move from his shoulder.

"Konstan, this is my daughter, Aiyra – though you probably know that by now. Aiyra, Konstan Marcel is an engineer; he works with Ms. Anselle. He also tends the birds," Marc added.

Aiyra cocked her head and looked inquisitively at Konstan. "Do engineers usually have birds. . . ?" she asked. Konstan laughed.

"No," he admitted. "I only take care of them because all of these birds are from Earth; and I'm the only one on this ship who was born and raised there. My parents were from Russia and Greece, to be specific."

"Oh. . ." said Aiyra thoughtfully. "I do not know where Earth is."

"It's in the next galaxy over," Konstan joked. "Seriously though, it's where most of us come from at some time or another; perhaps even you, Aiyra." He looked up at the ceiling, where a multi-colored glass cross was patterned. "Even He was born there." Aiyra followed his gaze.

"That must be wonderful to be born on Earth!" she said wistfully.

"It's wonderful just to be born, Aiyra," he replied, smiling.

Aiyra smiled back and reflected on his words a moment. "It is my birthday in a couple of days," she said thoughtfully. "I never had a birthday before; A'ma could not give me presents except a straw bracelet or doll sometimes, and the slave trade never stops for a birthday-" she looked up at the cross again. "Except maybe His."

Konstan looked at her with deepening respect. "Yes," he said softly, "Eventually every evil thing will stop because He was born.

Aiyra, that must have been awful for you! I hope you will have a wonderful birthday. Here-" He lifted the little dove from his shoulder.

"This little fellow is mine, rather, though all the rest are gifts. His name is Pyrrho; he was orphaned too, so I've taken care of him since he was a hatchling." He stroked the dove's wings. "I think maybe he would like it if you took care of him for me, Aiyra; that way he won't be around the noise of the other birds, which scares him." He nestled the dove in Aiyra's hands.

"Oh. . . Thank you!" she breathed, holding the now-cooing dove close. Aiyra looked up at Konstan. "I have never had a normal birthday before. What do you do for your birthday?"

Konstan frowned a little. "I don't, really," he admitted. "You see, I don't have a family."

"Oh! Why, you are like me – or, like I was," Aiyra said in surprise. She studied him for a moment. "Well, you can be my brother, then! And then whenever your birthday is, you'll have a nice one." A surprised smile tugged on Konstan's lips as he looked at her.

"That makes two," he laughed. "You and Samantha! Thank you, little sis. . . Now, be sure you have a great birthday!" He smiled at her and went to his work.

Aiyra and Marc watched him for a minute, as the boy fondled a few affection feathered friends and made sure they had enough to eat.

"Looks like you have a good friend, Aiyra," Marc said with satisfaction. "You can't have too many of those!" He didn't tell her that he had been hoping to have her meet Konstan, as he knew that Konstan's own loss of family might help Aiyra to deal with some of

her trauma. "Come on," he said lightly. "Your little dove needs a home."

Aiyra contemplated the dove which was now sleeping cradled in her hands. "Yes," she whispered, "And he has found one like I have." She held the dove to her cheek and they left the aviary.

~~~

An hour later the pair were sitting in Marc's cabin, watching the stars they passed. Little Pyrrho was happy in his new home after having been fed and watered, and after a joyful exploration of Aiyra's room, during which time he had discovered little Sage to be a nice, soft bed. And one that meowed, yawned, and decided that doves were fascinating little creatures, before promptly falling asleep again.

"So, A'da," said Aiyra, kneeling on the couch beside her father and looking mischievously into his eyes. "Tell me about yourself. Where are you from?"

Marc looked at her with a sad little smile. "It's a sad thing when a daughter has to ask her father to tell her about himself! But you were hardly three years old when they took you from me. . . Didn't you hear anything from your mother?"

Aiyra pulled gently at the chain around her father's neck, finding the cross of the Order which so fascinated her. "Yes," she said slowly, "but she did not know where you were from either." She looked up at him. "Are you from Earth, A'da?"

Marc smiled a little. "I don't know where I'm from, Aiyra. I was born on a space freighter in unclaimed territory, with no ties to anywhere; and my parents were of a long line of colonists who – well, never colonized. Eventually their country was forgotten."

Aiyra gently touched his face. "Is that why you love Cytha so much, A'da? Besides A'ma and I? Because it is your home?" Marc nodded and held her close.

"But they say home is where the heart is," he whispered. "I have half of it here; but the other half is still missing."

Aiyra did not answer for a minute. She knew her father's heart was still aching over the death of Talitha. She wouldn't want this, Aiyra knew. Her mother had loved them both so much that knowing this would, and surely did, hurt her.

"A'da. . . A'ma would say that you have all of your heart, right here," she said slowly, gently drawing his hand to her heart. "She gave me to you and took care of me all that time so that I might get back to you, A'da, with or without her. She gave everything for us, and she would not want you to hurt over it," she pleaded, struggling not to begin weeping herself. Marc did not answer, but held her close and wondered.

VIII

Shadows

The sky was lit golden by the rays of the sun, gilding the waves of the ocean which lapped on the shore. Roses spilled over ancient stone walls, and verdant hills rose in the distance. A few paradisaical birds sang in the trees.

"Oh, it is beautiful!" Aiyra breathed. "Where are we?"

"Same place as before," Konstan replied, laughing. "But this looks like Ireland, an Earth country."

Marc had sent Konstan to demonstrate to Aiyra the usefulness of the VR, or virtual reality recreation room. Konstan had been teaching Aiyra about Earth; she had seen Jerusalem and Rome, Constantinople and New York City, Antarctica and Africa, and now Ireland.

Now they seemed to be walking along the beach, feeling the waves wash over their feet. It seemed so real that Aiyra nearly walked into the wall of the room without realizing it.

"That's the unfortunate part," Konstan laughed. "It doesn't extend past reality!" He started to shut down the program, using his com-watch as a remote. At that moment, something dark and metallic seemed to shoot across the surface of the water and disappeared with such a horrid sound that Aiyra jumped in fright.

"Shut it off!" she begged him. Konstan was staring at the spot on the wall, perplexed.

"That's odd! What was that? It looked like a ship, but I'm pretty sure that's not in the program." Aiyra looked reluctantly around.

"It did," she sighed heavily.

Konstan frowned a little, wondering if one of the other engineers was playing a prank. "Come on, Aiyra, let's see if we can find the glitch."

He snapped off the VR and the beach vanished, revealing the spotless white room. Behind them was the bar, lounge, and board game room where disinterested personnel tended to spend their time guessing what 'those strange VR people' were looking at, rather than playing their games.

Konstan and Aiyra removed their headsets and entered the Tech Center. Samantha was, as usual, nowhere in sight, Aiyra noticed. Konstan pulled up the program on the VR computer and started taking it apart. Several minutes passed by as he stared at masses of figures and numbers. Aiyra's head hurt just looking at it, so she stepped behind him and waited.

"It doesn't seem to be here," Konstan said finally. "It's probably nothing." He looked up and saw Aiyra watching him. "What?"

"It looked like a Marauder ship," she whispered. Her eyes were clouded. Konstan stared at her a moment.

"Oh, Aiyra!" he sighed and getting up, he put his hands on her shoulders. "I'm sorry. . . You've been through a lot. Maybe we should avoid the VR until I figure out the glitch. . . okay?"

Aiyra drew a deep breath and smiled. "It is alright," she laughed softly. "I should not let it frighten me. I was on my own for so long, I had to learn to be strong and take care of myself. But now it is as if all that pain is coming back, now that I have someone to help me heal it. Especially now that I am not in a situation where the pain has to keep building up inside, and I have to hide it . . ." she paused. "Well, not much," she amended with a sigh. She glanced up at him with a sudden thought. "Konstan, have you ever hidden anything that hurt because you thought – that perhaps it might hurt someone else if you shared it?"

Konstan hesitated. He knew exactly what she meant, and he admitted that he had done so once or twice before. "But Aiyra," he said seriously, "Each time I learned that it would have done me good only if I had not hidden it. I can't go back in time now, and learn to trust that my parents would have hurt less over my secrets than over my secrecy. Aiyra, if you're hiding anything from someone who deserves to know, please realize that if they are unable to help you because of your silence, they may unintentionally hurt you." Aiyra's brow creased as she thought on this.

"I suppose you are right," she said at last. "Perhaps. . ." She seemed to forget him for a moment, then glanced up swiftly and smiled.

"Thank you. I will go now so that you can work." Konstan watched her leave, distractedly striking his hand with a screwdriver. He winced and commenced taking apart the computer to access the hard drive.

~~~

A faint humming sound was beginning to get on Marc's nerves as he walked around his desk to examine his intercom. The crackling of the speakers and the microphone had become worse, to the point at which his request for Aiyra's birthday cake was returned with an order of bacon and eggs. Marc had to admit to himself that he wasn't much of an expert when it came to fixing anything, so he went on a hunt for an intercom that was in working order. He finally found one way down the hall and put a call in to the Tech Center, crossing his fingers in the hopes that anyone but Samantha would be sent up.

"Good morning, sir!" Truitt's voice boomed over the speaker. Marc winced and hastily took a step away from the system. "What can I do for you?"

"The intercom system in my cabin is malfunctioning, specifically the speakers and the microphone," Marc answered, his ears still ringing. "I'd appreciate it if you could send someone to fix it in the next half-hour."

"I'm sorry, sir, but we're short on engineers," Truitt answered regretfully. "You know we always fine-tune the ship after we let off most of our passengers. I might be able to send someone shortly, but Samantha, Konstan, and the other engineers-on-call have task lists a mile long – literally," he added under his breath. "However, if you like, I'll try to rearrange the priority list and get someone there sooner."

Marc sighed and pushed his hair back. "That's alright, Truitt. It can wait. Thanks anyway." He hung up and stood there a moment, wondering why he always had technical difficulties whenever the engineers were busy. He gave up on the idea of ordering Aiyra's cake early and went back to his cabin to debate whether to buy her a dozen dresses or a pony, a dog, and an aquarium.

He was shocked out of his musings when a horrible noise came from the intercom and jerked him out of the chair. He frantically slammed his hand on the volume control and the noise vanished with an odd clinking sound that wasn't part of the static. Marc looked down and saw a familiar glint of ruby and gold somewhere deep in the crack of the control panel. He groaned. He must have been fingering his crucifix just a few moments before, and had loosened it from its cord.

"Great," he muttered, and, grabbing a random screwdriver that was deep in one of his desk drawers, started working at the top panel of the intercom. Unlike the intercoms found throughout the hallways of the ship, Marc's was built into his computer, which in turn was built into his desk. Thus, he had his work cut out trying to figure out what part of the machine was the computer, and what part was the intercom.

He had just taken a quick coffee break when the door suddenly slid open. He turned to see who had entered.

"Pyrrho!" he spluttered, as a ball of white feathers shot straight to his shoulder, and down went the coffee: straight into the mysterious depths of the computer's wiring. Aiyra appeared in the doorway, breathless, and looked to see her bird smoothing his ruffled feathers while on Marc's shoulder, and her father staring at the mess in dismay. He turned to look at the dove.

"Well, that was a real *pearl* of a timing!" he said sarcastically. The bird just squeaked and settled down under the collar of Marc's coat. The captain looked at his daughter. "What's up with this bird of yours?"

"Sage tried to teach him a lesson for eating out of her bowl, so he thinks that it is my fault that his perch turned into a scratching post," Aiyra apologized. "I will help you, A'da." Together father and daughter did their best to dry the wires and circuits they could reach, but it was rather useless.

"I wish I knew what to do with this now," sighed Marc, "but I'm no Konstan or Samantha." He blankly studied the inside of the computer.

Aiyra rested her head on her knee, examining the wires closest to her. "You should take out the battery if it has one," she suggested. Her father looked at her.

"I haven't the faintest idea what the battery looks like," he admitted. "But I'm thinking you maybe spend too much time around engineers!"

Aiyra looked troubled. "Maybe I have spent too much time around computers," she replied. "Sometimes . . . I had to know how they work. But those were ancient computers compared to these, so I do not really know anything about them."

Marc frowned.

"You never told me about that," he said gently. "Maybe you should?"

"Maybe later," she whispered. She shook her hair out of her eyes. "And maybe we should call Samantha or Konstan?"

Marc explained the situation with the engineers. There were a few moments of silence.

"A'da," the girl said at last, "what if I offer to help out with some of the computer tasks today? That might free up one of them to try and save the computer."

Her father didn't like the idea of his daughter working a job merely for the sake of his computer, but she insisted that she at least see if she could find either of them. Marc gave in on the condition that she put Pyrrho somewhere where he wouldn't be annoyed by the cat. The girl promptly ran out the door, laughing as she left her dove fast asleep on the captain's chair.

Marc shook his head and decided that it was pretty certain that, if either of the engineers were free enough for the job, it would be Konstan; after all, Samantha was older, more experienced, and thus her skill was in greater demand. He picked up a folder he had left on the desk to put it away, but a page slipped to the floor.

It was a picture of Talitha holding their daughter on her first birthday. Marc lost track of what he had been doing. He moved over to the window and became lost in thought. Minutes ticked by, and the stars glimmered as the *Lumenara* continued her peaceful journey to Maedra, the final destination for the remainder of the refugees. Marc felt as though each moment was an hour as he relived those all too few years with Talitha.

A sudden soft hiss broke his contemplation as the door slid open behind him. This time, it was not the heralding of a cat-and-bird fight. In fact, there was silence for several moments until Marc finally shook himself awake and turned to see the visitor.

It was Samantha. She stood motionless in the doorway of the brightly lit cabin, looking half-embarrassed. The silence continued. Marc saw the young woman's eyes go to the picture he still held in his hand, and knew she understood.

"Your wife was beautiful," she said softly. "Aiyra does look like her, doesn't she."

"Yes," Marc murmured, caressing Talitha's face with his eyes, then smiling a little. "Not to tie her down in her image . . . but in the mirror she can see her mother's gift every day and remember how much she loves her." He slipped the picture back into the folder. Samantha straightened.

"Aiyra told me your intercom is malfunctioning, and that you needed it, sir," the engineer said quietly. "May I?"

Marc blinked and put the folder aside. "How did she find you so quickly? I thought all the engineers had a heavy workload today."

Samantha laughed a bit. "It was, sir," she admitted, "until it was discovered that the computer systems seemed to be bypassing our manual locks and updating and reprogramming themselves to Vestar Fleet regulations. Don't ask me how because I wouldn't know."

She bent to look under the computer console at the fused wiring. It was a mess, just as Aiyra had described. She frowned, blew her hair out of her face, and started unscrewing the plexiglass plates that shielded the components, yet allowed for quick analyses. These Marc had left untouched, as he hadn't had the right tools for the job.

"At any rate, Aiyra's now with Konstan. He's showing her how to deal with fused wiring, which I have a feeling he could be doing right here," she said, her brow creasing as she examined the dark brown mess within the circuitry, and a mass of melted wires. "What exactly happened?"

"Eh . . ." Marc hesitated. "Well, you see – for the past few weeks I've been getting bugged by some interference that was coming over the com, and since Truitt told me we're short on engineers due to the fine-tuning of the ship, I figured I'd leave it." Samantha peered up at him. She raised an eyebrow.

"I have a feeling there's an interesting part you've left out regarding this mess. Please continue." She went back to work.

"Well, somebody gave me a call – well, more of a shriek– and when I jumped up to shut it off, my crucifix slipped into the panel; so I unscrewed it, but Aiyra's pet dove startled me and caused me to spill my coffee." Samantha stuck her head out from under the desk and stared at him with a suspicious frown.

"Ok . . . so you spilled your coffee and didn't even find the original problem. Nice." She ducked back under to get the last two screws. "The good news is, from what I can see the actual computer components have not been drowned, just drenched. I can't say the same for the intercom, but you likely needed new parts anyway." She pried the plexiglass off and set it aside.

"We're going to need isopropyl alcohol and distilled water-" she deftly removed the computer battery and set it aside. "-To remove the coffee from the parts. Now, in order to give each individual component a bath, we would have to take the entire computer apart and you would be left without a computer for quite some time. I recommend sending it back down to the Tech Center and getting a replacement. In the meantime, I'll work on the intercom." She found the computer hard drive, wiped it off on the skirt of her uniform, and handed it to him.

"Hopefully, you haven't lost anything on it." She peered into the computer again. "As for your crucifix, we'll likely find it when we work on this machine later on, tomorrow. I mean, today. No, probably tomorrow." She sighed and rubbed her forehead. "I should call Konstan," she muttered, beginning to untangle a few wires.

"Are you feeling alright, Ms. Anselle? You seem distracted," Marc noted.

Samantha sat up abruptly to answer, but hit her head on the edge of the desk. "Ouch!" she rubbed her forehead and glanced up with a wry smile. "Well, I was feeling alright until just then! I was up all night trying to unlock a computer server that decided to re-scramble its files every five minutes, plus I haven't had a chance to have coffee this morning." She plucked the tangled wires from the intercom and threw them away; they had been fused together.

"Now, if you weren't the captain, I might tell you to run and get me some coffee," she said, diving back under the computer. Her muffled voice continued, "But since you're the captain, I'll kindly ask you to please send for some instead."

Marc could tell she was laughing. Now it was his turn to shake his head, but he admitted that coffee didn't sound bad just then, especially since he had hardly gotten to taste it before the computer had polished it off. So, he paged the little cafe to send up some – before realizing that Samantha had just repaid him for the bump on the head. She sat up laughing now, managing not to hit her head this time, and looked at Marc's expression.

"Who's distracted?" she teased. "Me, or you? Who's the one testing an intercom system which is *obviously* not working?" She waved a screwdriver at him and disappeared again, still laughing. Marc found a smile tugging at his lips. He arose from his seat on the edge of the desk just as the door opened yet again. Aiyra bounced into the room, drawing a laughing Konstan along with her. The girl ran over to the desk and leaned over it, peering down at Samantha.

"Did she fix it?" she asked her father eagerly. Samantha poked her head out to look at her.

"Not yet! He needs a new computer. I'm working on the intercom now."

"Aw, I thought you would have fixed it by now," Aiyra said, playfully shoving Konstan as he prevented her from falling over the desk.

"And what happened to *your* workload, Konstan?" Marc asked, wondering just what had happened to that shortage of engineers.

"I've still got it," the boy laughed, "but Aiyra's quite good at fixing certain computer problems, specifically programming. Hey," he said, turning to his friend, "I ought to take you down to the Tech Center and have you take a look at the program on that computer. Unless it bothers you, of course."

Marc hadn't heard of the incident, so Konstan recounted it at his request, and admitted that he had had no luck finding a glitch anywhere in the program or in the computer.

"It's worth another look though. It may have been a type of direct-attack virus."

"Would someone mind explaining all these computer problems?" the captain demanded. "First, the VR computer, then the computer Samantha was working on last night, and now all the computers updating themselves when it's set to be manually controlled?"

"And then," Samantha added, climbing out of her cramped workplace at last, "there's that computer at the Academy of Design, which decided to take voice commands when it wasn't designed with the ability to do so."

Her eyes flickered to Aiyra, who was looking rather concerned about the chain of events. Konstan noticed as well.

"Hey, there's nothing to worry about, Aiyra. Don't let it bother you-"

Suddenly the intercom flashed on with the same horrible screech that Marc had heard earlier, just amplified. Everyone either jumped away from the intercom or scrambled to turn it off. Aiyra, who was closest to the machine, clutched her head and stumbled away.

"But I didn't even turn it on!" Samantha insisted. "And I fixed it!" She looked at Marc with a bewildered expression. "Perhaps I didn't fix it as well as I thought. It may be some sort of interference that's causing that particular shriek."

Marc quickly agreed. His daughter was trembling and clutching her head, which was still ringing like a belfry on Sunday. He went to her.

"Don't be scared, Princess! I know it sounded like the alarm the Marauders use when a prisoner escapes. . . it's alright. You're free now, and there's nothing for you to escape from anymore. You won't be hearing those alarms again."

Aiyra leaned her head on his shoulder, and he sent her to the couch with Pyrrho, who was recovering after the nasty shock.

Samantha and Konstan rechecked the intercom system and found nothing wrong with it. After placing a call to the Tech Center about a replacement computer, they prepared to leave. Konstan headed off to work on the ventilation on Level 9. Samantha was slower in leaving; pulling off her gloves, she studied Aiyra, who had fallen fast asleep with Pyrrho nestled against her cheek.

"Captain," she hesitated. She faced him. "I want to apologize for the way I acted a few weeks ago, after you told me your story. I didn't mean to take your trust for granted, or to hurt you. It's just that something has been a problem for me for a long time. . . Please understand."

Marc reached out and put his hand on the engineer's shoulder. Samantha finally raised her eyes to his face.

"It's alright, Samantha," Marc whispered. "As you told me once, I would never ask you to tell me anything if you did not wish to tell me freely. Whatever it is that is hurting you, if there is anything at all that I can do to make it easier for you, please ask." He hesitated.

"I'd move the stars for you if I could, Samantha, for all you've done for Aiyra, and for me. If you hadn't brought her out of the chapel when you did, it's more than likely she'd have been lost to me in that crowd of refugees."

Samantha let out her breath and smiled at him. "There were too many pieces of the puzzle in one spot," she said. "I'm just glad I was there to put them together. As for my problem-" she paused. "I wish I could tell you! But it would hurt you and Aiyra, and I'm afraid there's nothing that you could do for me, Captain. Thank you for understanding."

She turned to take her leave as two workers arrived to remove the computer. The engineer had not replaced the panels, as they would just have to be removed anyway. She glanced inside as the workers walked past, and saw a glint of red tangled with the wires.

"Oh!" she exclaimed, and darting forward, snatched up the crucifix just as Marc spotted it and reached for it.

"Ouch!" Marc grunted as they both bumped their heads, and they came up each holding one side of the cross. Samantha looked at it breathlessly and, handing it to him, took her leave. Aiyra abruptly sat up. Marc laughed.

"Have you been awake all this time, silly?" He gently tugged one of her many braids and she shook them out.

"Mostly," she admitted. "Aʹda, why is she hurting?"

"She didn't say. . . or couldn't. But from the fact that she thought it might hurt one of us, my only guess is that it has something to do with the Marauders. Possibly. I suppose there are other things that she might think could ruin a friendship."

He slid the crucifix back onto its cord and placed it around his neck again. Then he sat down beside his daughter, much to the disturbance of Pyrrho's nap. Aiyra laughed as the dove fluttered over to his newfound perch on the intercom, feathers all ruffled. Marc reached an arm around his daughter's shoulders.

"Now, let's talk about your birthday."

IX

Outbound

Morning came and found Marc and Aiyra strolling through Zaire, a bustling, yet quaint sea-city on one of Maedra's many ocean shores. Much to her father's surprise, Aiyra had decided to spend her birthday adjusting to normal life. Since Marc was supposed to visit Maedra to officially escort the last of the refugees down to the planet's surface, and since neither father nor daughter wanted to be parted, it worked out perfectly.

Maedra was beautiful, with lush valleys and picture-perfect oceans. Even the cities were more like a sprawling garden by the sea than the cities that Marc had visited previously.

The crew of the *Lumenara* were taking shifts, and spending their free time exploring the new scenery and breathing in the salt air.

At eight o'clock that morning, the governor of the region of Zaire met with Marc in the sunken plaza before the marble palace that sat on the water's edge, with its columns, fountains, and flowering shrubs and vines. The refugees who were with him found a warm homecoming as the entire city turned out to celebrate their freedom. Those who had been stolen from another time were shown just as much love, and given homes until the day that, perchance, they might return to their own homes.

Banners were flown, songs were sung, the trees festooned with ribbons and lights, and children darted through the crowd, laughing as they stole a little extra freedom from the care of their parents. The governor personally welcomed each refugee and then thanked Marc for his work in bringing them home. Konstan was there, and presented a pair of gorgeous birds-of-paradise to the governor as a gift, whereupon the entire crew of the *Lumenara* was invited to the celebration ball the following evening. All in all, it was quite the introduction to socialization and freedom for Aiyra, and quite a birthday party.

Father and daughter spent the remainder of that morning exploring each garden and fairytale alleyway they came across, studying the clouds, and buying things that Aiyra didn't need but that Marc wanted to give her. On one such occasion, as they came out of a quaint cobblestone alley draped with rose-colored flowers, with a beautiful silk shawl thrown over Aiyra's shoulders, a bouquet of roses and violets in her hands, a spray of crystal and enamel ocean waves in her hair, and a collection of old books in Marc's arms, they collided with Konstan and Samantha.

"Goodness!" laughed Samantha, as the books spilled and down went the roses. Konstan and Marc swept up the books as the engineer gathered the flowers and handed them to Aiyra.

"Happy birthday!" Samantha said. "I'm afraid I don't have a present for you at the moment, as Konstan and I were just about to start a hunt for one. Or two." She was laughingly eyeing the presents that Marc had already bought for his daughter, and wondered whether she could find anything that he hadn't found first.

Konstan leaned over and gave Aiyra a quick squeeze. "Happy birthday, princess!" He gently tugged on the bow in her hair. "I have a hunch by the time the day is over, you'll have so many presents you won't be able to find your bed," he joked.

"Seriously, though," Samantha interjected, "it's quite a birthday you're having, Aiyra! I hope it's alright." She studied her friend's face for signs of stress, but noted to her pleasure that Aiyra was quicker to adapt than she had expected. Clearly the girl was having the time of her life with her father, and her day was only made better by having her two friends with her as well.

"You look pretty, Samantha," Aiyra smiled. Indeed, on this rare occasion Samantha had traded her everyday olive-green and black uniform for a casual cranberry-colored utility dress over a plain cream-colored blouse and boots. Aiyra had a sudden idea.

"Please," she coaxed, "for my birthday present, can you spend the day with me? Both of you? You said yourselves I will get too many presents otherwise."

Konstan just laughed, and obviously liked the idea. He never had much luck when it came to birthday presents, anyway. Samantha, though, hesitated and glanced at Marc before giving in. Aiyra promptly led her off to the little marketplace outside the alley, where a troop of pet monkeys were causing mischief.

Marc and Konstan sat down on a low stone wall and watched the pair laugh as the monkeys danced and tried to eat Aiyra's roses. Konstan sighed and Marc turned his attention to him. The young engineer was watching Aiyra with a pained, grave expression.

"What's wrong?" the captain inquired.

"She's been through so much," Konstan murmured. "And she's so strong! So much stronger than I would be. I'm ashamed of myself for not having suffered as much nor as well as she has. True, I'm not in control of what God gives me to suffer, but couldn't I have suffered twice as well as I did? And even that would be nothing compared to

Aiyra. I can understand her because like her, I lost my whole family, yet she has you. We both spent most of our lives on our own, but she spent it in slavery, while I trained for the Vestar Fleet."

He sighed heavily, still watching the laughing girl, whom no one would have imagined as being a slave just five weeks before.

"I almost wish," he whispered, "that I could suffer more so that I could be like her. Captain, you're the most blessed father I've ever met, but I know you don't need me to tell you that."

Marc smiled softly, with a tinge of sadness mingled with pride. "Yes, I'm more blessed than I deserve; but I only wish that she could have been blessed with a mother always there at her side. If there were only Time. . ." He abruptly sank into deep thought, with an expression that caused Konstan to worry.

"Captain," he said quietly. "She can't come back."

Marc looked up. "No, she can't. But I *could find her.*"

"If you managed to make it through the fields of Borania, into the correct time, and were willing to save a woman who isn't quite your wife anymore," Konstan replied.

Marc bit his tongue.

"I know, sir, and I understand how you feel," Konstan said gently. "If I could go back in time, I'd try to save my parents. Yet I know that they wouldn't quite be my parents because I'd be preventing them, and God, from forming together the path that He planned from eternity. If you save Talitha, sir, she won't be the woman you remember. And you'll be *five* years older, at least, than she is. And if you try again to save her from being kidnapped in the first place, you'll be *fifteen* years older than her. And Aiyra. . . if you save the mother, you can't leave the child, sir. If you save Aiyra somewhere in time, then she won't be the girl you have today."

They both looked at Aiyra, who glanced back at them with laughing eyes and blew her father a kiss. Marc's heart was aching. What Konstan was saying made perfect sense. So then, if Talitha died. . . . Aiyra had been forced to watch her mother die, and had seen her buried. He groaned and knew that it was hopeless. His last chance of saving Talitha was gone.

When Aiyra had been returned to him, despite the story of her mother's death, Marc had received a faint flicker of hope that his wife could return to his side. But it was not his place to meddle with time any more than it was his place to say who should live and who should die. He sighed and looked at Konstan again.

"Thank you."

Konstan gave him a little smile as Aiyra danced up to them, Samantha trailing behind her.

"Where are we going now, A'da?" she inquired.

"Where would you like to go, sweetheart?"

Aiyra paused and her brow creased as she noticed his eyes. "Are you thinking about A'ma?" she asked softly, instead of answering. Marc just nodded. Aiyra looked at him, then at Konstan, who was frowning a little.

"We haven't lost her entirely, A'da," Aiyra said softly, turning back to him. "She is just in a different place, where you cannot reach her. She can still hear you; we will see her again, A'da."

Marc pulled her into his arms and held her close. Again, he knew she was right. He sighed, realizing once more how much of her mother was in her: her personality, her heart, everything. In fact, if he had Aiyra, whom Talitha had given life to and spent her own life, love, and energy nurturing her, was it not true that he still had Talitha in the sense that she had given him their daughter? Talitha had protected and comforted Aiyra through those seven years of slavery, in the hopes that father and daughter would be reunited.

He smiled into Aiyra's soft iridescent eyes, so much like Talitha's. Cythian eyes changed colors depending on one's emotions, surroundings, and even the colors they wore; now Aiyra's eyes were an aqua blue that mirrored the ocean waves.

"Come on, let's get your birthday going again." He took her hand and led the group towards the waterfront. A crowd of teenagers were gathered for a watercraft excursion. Spotting Konstan and Aiyra, and noting that they must be visitors as they were not wearing the native dress, the group waved to them and invited them to join the fun.

Aiyra looked at the water-speeders, which seemed quite fast compared to anything she had ever ridden. Konstan looked at them and thought how much fun his friend would have if he took her. Marc looked at them and saw that they would both enjoy the trip, and Samantha looked at Marc and noticed that he needed time to be able to shake off his mood and enjoy his daughter's birthday.

"Why don't you two take one of those water-speeders for a spin?" Marc suggested. As Samantha was thinking, it would give him some time to put sadness out of his head before his daughter returned. It would also give him a chance to talk to the engineer and see if he could somehow help her with her own problem, whatever it might be.

Konstan jumped at the idea, eager to show Aiyra a good time, and the pair ran down to the pier to join the group, though Konstan did have to coax her into speaking to the young people. Marc and Samantha went onto the balcony that overlooked the harbor.

The cool, salty breeze blew in their faces and tousled Samantha's dark hair. In a few moments, they saw Konstan and Aiyra's waterspeeder shoot out across the bay, leaving a sparkling spray of foam in its wake. A few curious seagulls chased them, while their other feathered friends came to Marc and Samantha, looking for a treat. Samantha laughed and tossed them the remainder of the cookie that she had been sharing with Konstan.

Marc leaned on the balustrade, breathing in the ocean air and watching as Konstan took Aiyra for a spin on the water. Behind them and across the bay was a cliff of white stone, stained a dark gray from ages of sea-storms, erosion, and ancient wars. The bay was several miles wide, with white-capped lapping waves of a blue so bright, it acted as a mirror to merge earth, sea, and sky.

Marc began to feel a nagging sense of fascination with the place, as if he had been somewhere like it before, and it held a story which he needed to be told. Samantha wandered down the colonnaded path parallel to the shore. Marc reluctantly followed, trying to place just what seemed so familiar. He shook himself out of his thoughts when the young engineer asked him a question about Aiyra's birthday.

No, Marc explained to her, it wasn't exactly Aiyra's *first* birthday celebration. In fact, Talitha had kept on trying to make the day special for her daughter, even in slavery. She wasn't able to do much, but every year she would weave a bracelet, a headband, a necklace, or some other little trinket so that Aiyra would know she was loved. Marc glanced down now and looked thoughtfully at the woven straw, leather, and seashell band that he wore under his coat cuff. Even on Cytha Talitha had made such little presents for the ones she loved.

"Ms. Anselle," he said slowly, pulling it off, "this was made by Talitha. . . I wish you would please take it." Samantha stared and looked like an alarm was going off in her ears.

"Why? I mean, your wife made it. I should think that you'd want to keep it."

"I think Talitha would want you to have it. . . she made it to comfort me when I was stressed one day. If she knew you, she would make one for you also. And I want you to remember that whatever it is that is frightening you, I'll protect you. A captain doesn't abandon even one member of his crew, Ms. Anselle, even an engineer who seems to be afraid of me."

His eyes were laughing a little, yet gravely looking into hers. Samantha reluctantly took the bracelet offered to her and they resumed their silent walk along the promenade.

They were passing a noisy, crowded hotel porch when a couple of young boys began bombing them with sandballs and the pair quickly ducked into a antique store's doorway, zig-zagged through the jumbled merchandise, and stumbled out into a silent plaza. The bubbling fountain looked ancient, and ivy tumbled tenaciously over the four walls surrounding the courtyard as if it had grown there for centuries. Weeds and wildflowers intermixed in the raised beds placed in the four corners of the walls, and popped up between the broken cobblestones. A lone pigeon sat high on the branch of a wild, climbing rose and preened itself.

"It looks as though no one has been here for ages," Samantha said in amazement, speaking in a whisper, for the air felt heavy with a silent presence. Marc approached the fountain, seeing a gleam of brass hiding beneath a patch of moss near its foot. He stooped and pulled the greenery away. Beneath lay an ancient marker, the inscription of which Marc read aloud.

In the year 1433, Earth Reckoning, the Lord of Maeldra was overthrown by way of his own tyranny. His people rebelled against him when he struck down the beloved of the city, a princess from many moons. Here marks the spot where she was first interred, before reburial in the cathedral that was later erected. Her death encouraged us to have the strength to buy freedom for our people, and our nation was cleansed and healed of the despot's curse.

This marker placed on the 50th anniversary of the death of the Lady Breciendelle, slave, mother, and queen,

May of 1483, A.D., E.R.

The wind whispered through the ivy leaves and scattered the broken petals of the rose, some falling into the fountain's still water. There were a few moments of silence.

"Well, that made little sense to me," Samantha confessed. "But whoever this lady is, she seems to be the only reason that Maedra is a happy place today. And now, I think we should be keeping an eye on your daughter, don't you?" She walked away, too disturbed by something she could not lay her finger on to remain any longer.

Marc lingered, staring at the light which glinted off the lettering on the marker. His eyes were slowly blinded as he fell deep into thought, and when he heard a soft footstep, he thought it was

Samantha. But for a brief moment he had the strangest feeling of being back in Cytha, with its gardens, fountains and courtyards, and his mind told him that it must be Talitha who was coming to see him. He shook himself out of his daydream and looked about, but his eyes were still too dazzled to see.

"Samantha?" he asked. There was no answer but the breeze. He must have been mistaken. He covered his eyes with his hand to adjust them to the dimmer lighting, and looked about again. This time he saw someone leaving swiftly through an archway in the far wall. He wondered if the man was visiting the marker as well. Perhaps he could explain the story it held. There was only one way to find out - he darted out of the courtyard.

X

Ruined

The salty ocean spray splashed Konstan and Aiyra as they zipped across the bay, the craft darting up over the crest of each wave and deep down into its valley. The wind whipped their faces as, laughing, they challenged one of the other teens to a race. They were having the time of their lives. No two had ever gotten along together as well as Aiyra and Konstan, it would seem, or so the other boys and girls observed. They were in harmony, and at times it was almost as though each instinctively knew what the other was going to say or do beforehand.

Eventually Konstan and Aiyra pulled away from the rest of the group with a mind to explore a bit, waving to their new friends as they sped off towards the cliffs.

"So," said Konstan, slowing down to a relaxing pace as the waves calmed, "how is your birthday so far, princess?" Aiyra laughed to hear him calling her by the same nickname her father used for her.

"It is very nice," she admitted. "I was afraid it would be too hard. I mean, not having my mother, yet having a real birthday, if you know what I mean. But I am so happy because I have my father. And now I have friends: you and Samantha." She looked around at the towering cliffs.

"I wish I had my mother," she said thoughtfully. "Yet I know she's still here with me, and she gave everything for me." She looked down at her hands and smiled to see a bracelet and ring woven of sea-grass and tiny seed pearls.

"See," she said, raising her hand. "A'ma made these for me on my last birthday before they killed her."

A shadow passed briefly over her face.

Konstan left one hand on the wheel, and leaning over, gently took her hand in his and glanced at the dual bands on her finger and wrist. He squeezed her fingers gently.

"Well, you have plenty of memories, Aiyra," he reminded her sympathetically. "Not the best, perhaps, as is only natural when you've spent almost your entire life as a slave."

"Mm," Aiyra agreed. "She always managed to give me good memories, though. She made my birthday seem special, and she never missed it, even if she was in pain. Oh, A'ma!" she breathed sorrowfully, and kissed the ring on her hand. They continued in silence for a while.

Konstan began teasing her and cracking jokes to make her smile, until she was laughing again. Now they were rounding a pillar of rock that stood in the middle of the bay. It looked almost as though it had been an ancient church steeple, but now it was overgrown with moss and dotted with the deep rose, lavender, and white of sea-lavender blossoms, and lilies floated on the water. Konstan brought the waterspeeder nearer to the rock.

Aiyra leaned out and gathered the white blossoms that floated upon the water, and the purple and pink buds that fell among the moss. Her gaze fell to the water as she stooped over it. While it acted like a mirror from a distance, here the water was clearer than crystal,

and Aiyra could see many fathoms below. Shapes lay there, half-buried, among rocks and coral. If she hadn't known better, she would have said that there was a fallen church wall, complete with a rose window, lying below her.

She paused and leaned closer to the water, noticed that the stones she was seeing scattered were arranged as though it had been a plaza long ago; yes, there was even a crushed fountain lying there, and a statue which seemed shockingly familiar despite the weathering on its face – Aiyra jerked back into her seat with a gasp and such a start that Konstan had to lean into her to balance the hovercraft.

"Aiyra?" Konstan asked, noting her wide eyes. Aiyra turned and looked out over the landscape around them. The bay was calm now, and the waves lapped against the narrow shoreline ahead of them, lying at the foot of those ancient cliffs. The girl leaned her head back and stared at the uneven summit. A low moan escaped her lips.

Konstan thought she was ill, and hastily put an arm around her. "Aiyra, what is it? What's wrong? Do you want me to take you back?" Aiyra leaned against him and took a few moments to answer.

"No," she whispered. "I need to go up the cliffs, Konstan." She raised her eyes to his face. "Please?" The youth hesitated, glancing behind them at the harbor.

"Alright," he said finally. "But I'll call Samantha and let her know. Are you sure you're alright?" The girl looked at him.

"I will be. Like I always have to be."

With a frown, Konstan called his friend on his com watch. There were a few beeps, and then Samantha's voice finally came over it.

"Hey there, little brother. What's up?"

"Aiyra needs me to take her up the cliffs for something," he replied. "Let the captain know, please, if you're still together." There was a moment's pause.

"We were together," Samantha answered finally, "until just a minute ago. I left him in a courtyard, and I thought he would be coming along in a minute, but he's gone now. Look, I'm heading back to the harbor so I can keep an eye out for both of you. I'll call him as soon as I can pick up the signal on his watch. Be careful, both of you!" she warned. "I know he trusts you, Konstan, but going up the cliffs is a little more than I think he'd like."

"I have to go," Aiyra repeated. "Please, Konstan. Ada will understand why when I tell him. I *have* to." Konstan sighed and relayed the message.

"I'll have her back in about an hour," he told the engineer. "See you later, sis." He snapped it off and turned to Aiyra. He looked at her for a few seconds, and seeing that she would not change her mind, started up the motor and took her to the shoreline.

Twenty minutes later, having found a rocky path lined with bright tumbling hidara flowers on the other side of the headland, the pair found themselves at the top of the cliffs. The wind was strong here, and whipped Aiyra's dark hair around her face as they looked out over the bay for a few moments. Then Aiyra turned and struggled down the remnants of a wide pathway.

It seemed that this headland used to be crowned with a low wall and cobblestone pavement, with a raised dais that had crumbled into the sea. Now straggling olive trees and seagrass strangled the ruins, and birds made their nests in the cracks of the walls. Then rose before them the weathered form of a castle. It had been so eroded and buffeted by the waves, and evidently torn by fire and storm, that it seemed to have sprouted from and fallen back into the cliffs themselves.

Aiyra took no notice of fallen statues and cracked columns, but struggled through hanging vines and over collapsing walls as though she had passed that way many times before. These seemed to be the ruins of ancient hanging gardens. Unknown herbs and flowers grew recklessly wherever they could among the stones. Konstan followed her swiftly, wishing she would slow down lest she hurt herself, and trying to clear some of the swinging vines to make the return journey a little easier.

After several minutes, he finally caught up to her in the looming shadow of a ruined throne room that overlooked the sea. The glass was missing from the windows, and patches of the sky could be seen through the collapsing roof. Mosaics were half-hidden beneath centuries of dirt and dust, and threadbare tapestries clung to the walls, their tatters blown in the breeze. A weather-beaten throne stood at the far end of the hall, and just a few paces before it stood a statue of a soldier, as if thrusting his sword into an enemy pinned at his feet.

Aiyra halted and stared at this statue. The waves roared faintly below them. Slowly, hesitating every step, the girl went forward and looked at the sword's blade, for it was real. A dark stain remained there, as though it had begun to rust, or perhaps it had been used to strike and not been cleansed. . . .

Minutes ticked by. Aiyra did not move. Konstan anxiously touched her shoulder. She jumped in shock and stared into his eyes, her breath now coming rapidly as if she had run up the cliffs.

"Aiyra! What is it?" The girl drew a shaky breath. She choked.

"They killed my mother here!"

XI

Vision

"They called the planet Aliros," Aiyra sighed. They were sitting on the edge of the dais, with the wind blowing through the empty windows as they stared at the statue. Konstan had filled two ancient glasses with water from a spring well outside, and Aiyra found it useful for hiding her shaking hands. She looked down into her glass for a moment.

"It was a mining planet," she explained. "The radioactive crystals found in these cliffs were used to power the Marauders' ships; that is, they probably still use them. It is odd to think that I still exist back then. . . how many times did I have to work with the other slaves to load the cargo bays with crystal?" She sighed again and dumped out the rest of her glass.

"Every day was spent in the dark, slimy cold of the mines, with only the phosphorescence of the crystals to light the caves. The work was painful, hard, and dangerous, of course, since we had little to no protection from radiation. Anyway, my mother was kept at home – if you could call it home - working to tend the ills and aches of the nobles in the apothecary. Occasionally Lord Daruth would come down to see that everything was in order. Eventually his visits became too often; he started asking her to visit him, or walk with him, but my mother tried to refuse."

"Finally, when my mother declined his offer of marriage, explaining that she was still married, he seemed to give up on the idea. My mother was beloved by all of the slaves, for there was no one kinder despite her own condition, and she spent every moment working to make their lives a little better. They called her a queen," Aiyra smiled sadly. "She should have been!"

"But what happened? Why did they kill her?" Konstan asked. Aiyra let out a shaky breath and shook her head.

"Daruth had a wrath that made all fear him. . . he summoned my mother and I before him and tried again to force her to give in. He even tried to place the crown on her head, which seemed odd, and my mother would not let it touch her. Just as he grew angriest, my father had reached the palace gates; and the guards fought with him and threw him out as Daruth-" Aiyra paused with a shudder.

"He ran down from the dais and snatched the sword from the statue," she whispered, raising her eyes to see the dull blade before her, her eyes glazed as if she were seeing the moment pass before her as a ghostly vision. A dull ache began in her neck and her head began to throb with a distant memory. In one instant, it flashed before her as though the curtain of time had been torn –

Her mother thrown down at the statue's foot –

Her father thrown down from the palace and lost to time –

Her mother's insistent plea for her daughter not to fear –

Her father's scream of anguish and the blood-red wrath in Daruth's eyes –

And the sword blade which struck her mother down before it clattered on the stone.

And he killed her before I got to say good-bye.

Aiyra blinked then and found herself on her feet, supported by Konstan. There was no Daruth, but her mother's cry and her father's scream lingered in her ears. All else was silent but for the wind in the tapestries and her gasping breath. Slowly the agonizing pain in her head subsided.

"Aiyra. . . Aiyra, are you going to be alright?" Konstan whispered anxiously, looking down into her pale face.

The girl straightened as all the emotion drained from her face, leaving her numb but capable. She looked up. A very faint smile tugged on her lips.

"As I said. . . I will be fine. Like I always have to be. I found my mother's place at last; and so have I found my father. Let us go. Thank you for bringing me here." Konstan looked down at her and wished that he had not complied with her request. He took her arm and they left the cliffs and the softly moaning ruins behind them.

~~~

Marc ran along the sidewalk as horses, scooters, and hovercraft swiftly passed him by. Just ahead of him he kept catching glimpses of the dappled gray cloak, so conspicuous among the brightly colored garments of the citizens, like a wreath of mist on a field of wildflowers. The sun was climbing high in the sky, overcoming the cool breeze so that Marc was drenched with perspiration by the time he stumbled into the shade of the church spire. The cathedral looked as though it had been constructed of rays of moonlight, frozen in time; and wisteria was woven throughout, climbing over its walls as though on a trellis.

Marc paused, breathless, and glanced in every direction. Strangely, the street here was empty, as was every garden, courtyard, and alleyway. He glanced up at the cathedral door, crowned with a set of seven stars. Unless his quarry had entered the church, Marc had lost the trail. He wondered briefly why he had even been following him. He shook off the strange feelings he had been having since setting foot on the planet, and slipped inside.

Here it was dim and cool. He moved down the nave, lined with slender columns of gray and silver; the walls of white stone, pierced with stained-glass windows, blocked out any noise from the outside world and filtered the light. Shafts of vermilion and sapphire, gold and violet fell over Marc as he crossed the nave and glanced into the side chapels, dotted with candles, carvings of wave-like motifs, and statues painted in gentle hues. There was no one to be seen but a lone priest, kneeling at an altar dedicated to the Virgin.

Marc went on, and crossed into the main aisle of the church. He was studying the marble and mosaic floor when a whisper caught his ears and he looked up. At first, all he saw was the tabernacle, with its winged angels and silvery curtain. His eyes went to the altar. There the gray-clad figure stood before the gate to the sanctuary, blending in with the stones and shadows. One beam of light caught on the cloak's hood.

Marc stopped. A shiver crept up his spine and he began to feel that it was more than curiosity that had drawn him to follow this daytime shadow. He drew closer, but dared not pass the last pew. Seconds – or was it minutes? – ticked by as he waited tensely for the figure to turn.

A bell struck somewhere high above them, tolling thrice. A chorus of birdsong followed, as though their voices had been trapped inside the bell; but there were no birds to be seen, and their song could not have lifted so high as to be heard within the sturdy walls of the cathedral. The hood fell from the figure's head, revealing thick brown tresses twined with a golden thread, and she turned to face him. In that one moment it was as if all time stood still. Marc's heart seemed to stop with it.

"*Talitha!*" he gasped when he found his voice. The woman smiled, half-sadly. Marc stared a moment longer, then leapt forward to hold her.

"No!"

Marc jerked to a stop, eyes wide, as Talitha stepped away from him, now with her back towards one of the side archways leading outside. She looked at him tenderly.

"My love. . ." she murmured. "You must not touch me."

"Why?! Talitha, *don't do this to me!* I've found you, and I'm not letting you go!" He took a step closer, but Talitha watched him warily.

"Marc, you must understand. . . *noli me tángere*. I have come not to be with you, but to warn you. You must not try to save me!" Her voice was urgent, and her eyes searched his, begging him to understand. "If you save me, my love, each human being on this planet will die, and Aiyra will no longer be ours. She will be destroyed in a way worse than death. If I do not die, the lord who once was of this planet will force my will. . . and then our daughter will perish at his command."

Marc's eyes widened again. His heart began to ache so that he could scarcely stand. He leaned against the communion rail and looked at his wife. She was more beautiful than he remembered.

"Then it was you," he whispered. "You are the one they called Breciendelle! But are you real?"

She only smiled. "Marc. . . do not fear. You will see me again, indeed, sooner than you think." Marc looked bewildered. Talitha laughed softly.

"You will find me, Marc, but you must not save me. That is why I must warn you! You will be tempted. . . the fate of a galaxy shall rest on your shoulders in that moment, and you must know my wish and the wish of the God who made us both. Do not save me, Marc. My fate was not your fault, but His Will; you could not have done more for Aiyra and I than you have done. Be at peace! I died willingly for Aiyra, for you, for them. And now, there is one who needs you much more than I, my love. . ."

She studied his face, a soft light in her eyes. She reached out and gently brushed his hair back with her hand, then kissed his brow.

"Let me go. . . let me go, as you must. You have done all you can for me, as you always have. Now, help me to help them."

Marc began to weep, looking into the eyes of his beloved, and knew she was beyond his reach. Konstan and Aiyra had been right. Talitha stepped back.

"Be at peace!" she breathed. She lifted her hood once more. Marc jumped forward, but stumbled into a shaft of light so bright that he was blinded once more. When he had blinked away the shadows, Talitha was nowhere to be seen. He was left with confusion as to whether it was a dream, a vision, or a hallucination. But directly in front of him was a painting of the resurrected Christ and Mary Magdalene, and before it, in the doorway, stood Samantha and Aiyra.

They were looking at him, Samantha in curiosity, and Aiyra with a silent look that told him she already knew. All three paused a moment. Then Marc leapt forward and drew Aiyra into his arms.

The last hour replayed in his head again in a rush as his tears wet Aiyra's hair. Samantha hung back until Marc sensed that Aiyra, too, was in shock. The engineer related the story given her by Konstan.

Marc looked again at his daughter. The happy sparkle in her eyes was no longer there, as was to be expected; but her face and bearing had changed, as though she was once again the tough girl who had born five years of slavery alone. He stooped and kissed her forehead with an aching heart.

"Come, darling," he whispered. "We'll find your mother now." He put his arm around her and led her to the priest who was still kneeling at the little side-altar. The priest looked up.

"Father, where was the body of the Lady Breciendelle laid?" Something in his face made the priest arise and lead the captain through the nave of the cathedral down into the crypt. A flight of upward stairs opened upon a blaze of stained-glass windows in a secret chapel, where the colored light fell softly upon an elegant casket surrounded by roses and violets. The effigy of the lady was carved upon its lid in lifelike relief. Marc took one longing look at it and fell upon it.

XII

Guidance

Aiyra swept down the hall towards the lobby on the engineering level. It was mid-afternoon; Samantha had returned with them to the ship after several hours of painful prayer in the crypt. Aiyra had left her exhausted father asleep at his desk, and was hunting for her friend. She found her seated on the floor of the lobby, rewiring an intercom system. Aiyra sat cross-legged beside her. Samantha stopped and returned the girl's steady gaze.

"You doing okay?" she asked wearily, flipping a lock of hair out of her eyes.

"Too many memories."

"I know, Aiyra; I know!" Samantha sighed, putting away her wire cutters and freeing her goggles from their perch on her dark hair. "I wish it hadn't happened on your birthday, of all days. In the very least, you know now where your mother is, and you can visit her. I haven't seen my mother in years, either." She paused to remove her gloves. They sat in silence for a few seconds.

"I need a mother," Aiyra said abruptly, "but she is gone. Samantha, I need you to be my sister." Her eyes were grave and earnest. Samantha mentally compared her to the Aiyra she had known, and wondered if the change would last.

"If it helps you heal, Aiyra, I'd be honored to be your older sister. First things first: you need to realize that, given the little I heard of Marc's experience, your mother is safe and happy. She does not want

99

you to hurt like this, Aiyra! She wants you and your father to be yourselves, not living ghosts."

Aiyra smiled a little. "You sound like me talking to my father! See, we are similar already."

"Don't change the subject!" Samantha teased. "Promise me that you understand the good of this, Aiyra. You have already experienced the whole thing; I fully understand that memories can refresh the pain, especially being in . . . well, almost a haunted place. You watched your mother die five years ago; and at last, you can visit and tend her burial place. You know how much she is loved by the people of Maedra for inspiring their freedom; you know that she is safe and happy, and that she loves you. What is more, you have your father! Aiyra, don't let this shape you more than God desires."

Aiyra's eyes were laughing now, and the weight seemed to have left her shoulders. "You always tell me what I need to hear, especially if it is something I already know," she told her. "I seem to need an outside source to tell me that I am thinking properly. Thank you, Sahma!" She rose to go.

"Hang on – how's your father?"

Aiyra stopped and looked back over her shoulder with a mischievous smile.

"I will help him be alright! Do not worry, Sahma. He is just exhausted; deep down, he was still hoping to save my mother. But now, seeing her, hearing her, and visiting her grave has wiped that hope away. I will take care of him, though." With a little laugh, she turned and exited, leaving a rather bewildered engineer behind.

~~~

Aiyra knelt beside her father in the chapel and laid her hand on his arm. He was leaning on the communion rail, his head in his hands.

"A'da?"

He stirred, but did not answer except to cover her hand with one of his. The chapel was quiet save for the faint humming of the lights overhead and behind the stained-glass windows. Marc raised his head.

"We can bring her flowers now," he said.

"Mm." Aiyra laid her head on his shoulder. "I am glad we found her, A'da, even if it did make it a sad day. We can visit her now; she would like that."

"Hm, lots of people visit her, darling," Marc replied, still gazing wearily at the tabernacle. "They loved her. . . remember the plaque I showed you in the courtyard?" Aiyra nodded.

"Do you know why they called her a queen, A'da?" She pushed away the thought of her father's presence that day, as a chill crept up her spine and pricked her temples.

"Yes; she would have been the queen of Cytha." Aiyra stared.

"But – then – but they called her that because she was almost a queen for them because she loved them." Marc glanced at her.

"But didn't your mother tell you she *was* a queen? Would have been, I mean," he corrected himself. Aiyra slowly shook her head. She looked thoughtfully at the ring on her hand.

"But then. . . you would have been king," she said softly, looking up into Marc's restless eyes.

"Maybe."

"And I would be a princess," she added slowly. "A'da, what happened to our people?"

"Most of them were enslaved or killed that day," Marc replied. "Some of them escaped to the star Alnilam in the third quadrant of the great Galaxy, where they are out of reach of the Marauders." He smiled a little, knowing what his daughter would say next.

"And yes, I know you now want to go to them, and we will, but not yet. We'll stay with your mother for now." Aiyra nodded, feeling that this was a good decision.

"But A'da, I thought the Marauders never went beyond the borders of Andromeda."

"Cytha was the farthest the Marauders had ever dared to penetrate the Milky Way," he answered grimly. "It was their first attempt, and their last. They have not tried since, for our retaliation was too great." His face hardened and Aiyra knew instinctively that he had led the retaliation once he had returned to his own time.

"Oh, Aiyra!" Marc murmured, shaking himself and holding her close. "Of all the days. . . I'm sorry about your birthday, dearest. It's going to be hard for a while, but as you say. . . your mother would want us to be happy. And we don't have all that much of a new cause to be unhappy. We'll celebrate your birthday tomorrow if that's alright."

"But there is the governor's welcome celebration tomorrow," his daughter reminded him. "You have to attend."

"Well, that doesn't mean you can't!" Marc smiled, remembering then that they were still in the chapel. He started to arise, but Aiyra gently tugged him down.

"He likes it when we tell Him about normal things, too," she smiled. "And we are alone, anyway." They prayed for a little while, as night fell on Maedra, and the waves lapped below the *Lumenara*, docked at the Zaire spaceport. The moon glinted on the walls of the church in the distance, and one could have sworn they saw a figure wrapped in the light; but it faded away with the wind.

XIII

Nightmares

Marc was having a nightmare. He was standing upon the cliffs and looking down into the depths of the ocean below. He heard a rasp of metal, as of a sword being drawn behind him, but he couldn't move – then the sea rippled, and he saw the face of Talitha, calling his name as if from a distance. There was a rush of footsteps behind him, and Talitha's cry–

"No!" Marc tried to scream, but the wind tore it from his lungs and carried it far away, and still he was bound to the rock beneath his feet. Talitha's image vanished from his sight. He heard Aiyra weeping, and then the water began to rage below him. It opened into a gaping mouth, a whirlpool with depths of swirling colors like faded time – Suddenly the cliff began to crumble, pitching him helplessly towards his grave.

"A'da! A'ma!" came a faint wail from behind him, but it was cut off when the pit prepared to swallow him -

"No! *Talitha! AIYRA!*" Marc jolted upright, shaking and drenched in cold sweat. He looked wildly around at his surroundings, then realized that he was still in bed. The only light in the cabin was the moonlight reflecting off the water below, and the dim amethyst glow of the lights on his intercom and computer.

All was quiet. Marc breathed a sigh of relief and got up, pulling on his coat and boots. It was nearing midnight, the time he usually headed to the chapel in case he missed his morning prayers later. He slipped into Aiyra's room, hoping he hadn't woken her. He froze. Something was wrong – both Aiyra's bedroom door and the door to her cabin were ajar, and her bedsheets lay tangled on the floor.

He ran out into the corridor. His daughter was nowhere to be seen. The one place she was likely to be was the chapel, and he was heading there already. He sprinted to the elevators.

Five minutes' time found him peering into the chapel and realizing that Aiyra had not, in fact, headed to her favorite place on the *Lumenara*. There was only one other obvious possibility: wherever Samantha was, Aiyra was sure to be around. Having not the faintest idea whether Samantha was asleep or working late, nor knowing where her cabin was, Marc started in the general direction of the engineering deck on the IT level. He might find her in one of the lobbies or recreation rooms, he thought.

All was still as he entered the deck. The lights were on, but dimmed. A few technicians were still monitoring the ship's systems, but they did not notice him pass by. Marc rounded a corner in the lobby and nearly crashed into Konstan. The boy's eyes went wide with surprise.

"Oh, there you are, Captain –Aiyra's with Samantha," he called over his shoulder as he darted away.

"But where is-" Marc began, and muttered impatiently under his breath when he realized the boy was already out of earshot. Remembering how anxious the young engineer had looked, Marc figured something was very wrong. He ran down the next passageway, lined with dorm rooms, and punched Samantha's number into the nearest intercom. There was a crackle, and then Truitt's voice came over.

"Yes, sir?"

"What, I want Samantha," Marc replied in frustration.

"I'm here with her now, sir, and your daughter's here, too."

"Well, where's here?" he demanded.

"Lobby #427, sir." Marc slammed his fist on the off button and winced as he heard a crunch of plastic.

"Those cheesy things," he muttered, and sprinted to the next junction of corridors. He became confused by the numbering and room directions, and it took him nearly five minutes to figure out that the lobby he was looking for was located at the end of the first hall he had been in. He pushed open the frosted glass doors and stopped short.

Samantha was standing there, holding Aiyra in her arms; and the girl was pale enough to have fainted. But Samantha was softly singing in a language he had hardly heard before, soft and sweet. Truitt, who was standing nearby, motioned for the captain not to interrupt the song. It was well that he did not, for Aiyra soon became quiet, listening to her friend's voice.

"Aiyra!" Marc breathed. He touched his daughter's shoulder. "Aiyra, what is it? Did you have a nightmare?"

She nodded, then shook her head. "I was dreaming about working in the mines again, but then I heard A'ma calling," she whispered. "I followed her voice, but I only found Samantha."

"The poor lass is hurting so much, she's making herself ill," Truitt added.

"Oh, my baby girl!" was all that Marc said, and he held her until her tears stopped coming. "You'll be okay. . . your mother loves you. Even though you didn't see her, you heard her voice. She must have had a reason for bringing you to Samantha, dear. Maybe because she's the only woman friend you have, and perhaps she can help you heal better than I." Aiyra sighed and shook her head. She had stopped shaking, but her father had to support her.

"You needed to see A'ma," she said wearily. "Because you only had her for a little while, and I had her longer. And she is the only one who could heal *you* A'da." She straightened and carefully shook her curls over her shoulders. She looked for a second at Marc's crucifix, which he had begun to wear openly.

"I will be alright now, A'da." Turning, the girl murmured a thank you to Samantha and Truitt. Konstan slipped back into the lobby, little Sage on his shoulder. Konstan took Aiyra's hand, laying the tiny purring bundle in her arms, and offered to help Marc take her back to her room. Marc accepted, and moved to follow them out.

"Captain!" Samantha stepped forward, and Marc stopped as the door shut behind Konstan and Aiyra. He looked back at her. The engineer hesitated. She looked different to Marc's eyes; probably because she was wearing a soft gown, the color of cherry blossoms, with beaded flowers. It was much more feminine than the structured uniforms she generally wore, but her troubled expression was the same as the one he had seen when she had first mentioned her problem to him. Samantha looked up again.

"I think she's hiding something from you," she said quietly.

"Who, Aiyra?"

Nodding, Samantha added, "I know she's been hiding at least some physical problems – I don't know if she told you." When Marc shook his head, the engineer sighed. "I told her she ought to tell you! So did Dr. Menendez. But Captain, something is causing Aiyra to swing from sweet and childlike one moment, to a strong, capable girl the next, and a frightened, melancholic one a moment later. It's quite possibly caused by trauma."

"You think that it's something that happened to her," Marc said softly, "and which she hasn't told us?"

Samantha nodded. "I wouldn't put anything past the Marauders! I've had more to do with them than you know, Captain. I might be able to help. . ."

She hesitated again and glanced at him. Marc had no idea that she was measuring his strength in aiding Aiyra's problems to date; and that she was realizing that he was the only one she could trust, and that he trusted her.

Marc's eyes softened. "Your problem. . . ?" The engineer smiled faintly and nodded. "Tell me, Samantha," Marc requested. Reaching out, he gently took one of her hands in his. "I'll help you. Sit with Aiyra and I at breakfast; it'll do both of you good. You can tell me everything, and then we'll see if we can help Aiyra."

Samantha looked almost relieved and thanked him. Marc turned to leave again, but Samantha's hand lingered in his. Truitt pretended not to notice; Marc slipped out and found Konstan and Aiyra waiting for him. As it was nearly one in the morning, he sent Konstan off to bed and carried Aiyra to the elevator. They rode in silence, with just the humming of the hydraulics keeping them company.

"Aiyra, is there anything you want to tell me?" Marc whispered at last. Aiyra, nearly asleep, stirred.

"Just one thing," she mumbled. "I should have told you, A'da. . ." Marc looked down at his sleeping child and knew it would be a long night.

"Please don't let it be much!" he breathed.

XIV

Marked

Morning finally came, but the day proved to be too busy for Samantha to join Marc and Aiyra at breakfast. The air conditioning system was having problems again, which broke out in the weirdest places: the restaurants' kitchens, the laundry facilities, and the aviary. Konstan was absorbed with trying to keep his birds from overheating, while the restaurants were forced to forgo the usual hot breakfasts in favor of smoothies, cold bacon from last night's BLT's, and some sort of banana pie that no one could remember baking.

Breakfast – or the little there was of it – was interrupted before Marc could inquire of Aiyra just what she thought she should have told him. Someone accidentally rerouted all the water from the emergency sprinkler system, and the air conditioning vents all over the ship began to leak; unfortunately, whoever had designed the ship had not thought of avoiding placing vents over computers and other electronics. The ship's data banks were half-deleted; thankfully, Marc had thought to copy the most important files to his own computer.

He soon found himself shepherded down to the *Lumenara's* reactor room, where he teamed up with Samantha to attempt to transfer and restore all the files and missing data. Engineers and technicians darted in and out, until the air conditioning system was under control and they had to take on the task of fixing every bit of electronics that had been rained on. This left Marc and Samantha alone with the beeping, stalling computers. Lights flashed as the systems tried to download and reabsorb the information.

For a long time, Samantha strained her eyes, staring at the computer screen and trying to make sure that everything worked; Marc's neck started to ache after many minutes of bending over a data console and downloading file after file. Eventually, both just stared at the screen as the computer decided to slowly begin doing its job.

"Ms. Anselle," Marc said at last.

"Mm."

"Recall that we were to have a conversation this morning."

"I'd rather not, sir, if that's alright.... I don't think I can really tell you." There was a pause. Samantha wished she had never said she'd tell him. The seconds ticked by as she felt Marc's confused gaze while she stared unseeingly at the computer screen.

Why was she doing this? She could trust Marc, she needed to tell someone – he was gentle and he could help her. Why didn't she say something!

"Ms. Anselle, may I ask you an odd question?"

"Mm."

"....Do you love me?"

The engineer froze. "That's... what I call an odd question!" With a sudden lightheaded feeling, Samantha pretended to work on the computer, which needed no help at all.

"That still doesn't answer my question." Marc smiled quietly to himself, still staring at the console. A minute ticked by. "If you don't answer, I'll know what your answer is," he gently reminded her.

"Oh, Captain, please, not right now – I'm trying to work!" came the flustered reply. Marc gave up. He went and put his hands on her shoulders.

"Samantha, it's alright! I'm not angry with you. I'm just trying to solve our rather awkward relationship."

Samantha almost laughed. "I suppose it is," she admitted.

Marc sat down next to her.

"Look – just because I've been married before and happen to be – what, seven years older than you? Doesn't mean that it's odd for you to love me. . . or for me to love you."

Samantha blinked, looked at him, then instantly blushed and got up to fiddle with the computer's wiring.

"Careful! Let's not add to our workload," Marc warned her just in time. She realized what she was doing and hastily dropped the wire, which would have snapped off the filing process at an inopportune moment. Marc gently caught her hands and pulled her away from the computer.

"Captain!" Samantha remonstrated, and tugged her hands away. "Please don't! I don't want anyone to think wrongly of you. . . not that my idea of why would make sense." She shook her head.

"Samantha, please, can't you tell me what's hurting you now? I want to be here for you the way I wasn't allowed to be for Talitha." Marc searched her green eyes. "If you don't want me to love you, I won't; but you can't ask me not to help you. Can you trust me?"

Samantha looked up at him. "I can trust you," she whispered, "but I'm afraid to tell you!"

"You already told me it was regarding the Marauders," Marc soothed her. "That hasn't turned me away, has it?" Samantha smiled faintly.

"If I tell you–you won't think the same way about me, Captain," she whispered. "I – I don't want that to change. And yet–" she shook her head. "Oh, if it will prove to you why you can't love me!"

Marc's patient, amused expression simply read, *good luck.* Samantha took a deep breath.

"A long time ago – eighteen years, just before Almedra was destroyed – I used to love sitting down by the lake near our village, alone. I shouldn't have," she admitted. "My father used to warn me not to go too far alone because of the history with the slave trade. But I was always the kind of girl who wanted, yes, *needed* the freedom the world would not allow me to have. Unfortunately, I finally learned my lesson – or rather, the world decided to put its chains on me."

"What happened?" Marc inquired when the engineer stopped. Samantha shrugged helplessly.

"An old man and his grandson found my favorite place; I was drawing the lake at the time," she remembered. "The boy's grandfather was of a rather veiled, cruel sort, but the boy and I became friends. We met often by the lake after that, as he was on vacation. He told me that people had been hurting him; that no one loved him. I felt sorry for him, of course, and because I found him to be a good friend, I did what I could for him. But when the time came for him to leave for his home–" She stopped again. It took some encouragement from Marc for her to continue.

The boy had run down to the lake to find her, but seeing that she wasn't there, came to the village church (where he had never been before, and a fact which should have been a warning sign, Samantha noted). He had told her that he was grateful for her friendship, and that he hoped that he would see her again; but it wasn't too likely except for one thing. Reaching up, he had pricked himself on the sword of St. Michael.

"And he proceeded to mark my forehead with the Marauder's symbol," Samantha murmured, staring at the floor as if she were feeling the mark all over again. "He was Medrhos, the heir to the slave empire. . . his grandfather wasn't there on vacation, but as a scout to choose the Marauders' next victims. It was shortly thereafter that our planet ended up being destroyed by the meteor." She looked up at Marc with pleading eyes.

"Can you understand now?" she begged him. "The scar he gave me is a danger to everyone I love! He promised to return and take me away, whether I wished to go or not; and anyone whom I love, or who loves me, will be in his way. He'll do anything to them if he finds me! That is why I told you it would hurt you and Aiyra. You must pretend there is nothing but friendship between us, Captain. Please. . .He's ruthless, unpredictable, and always two steps ahead. There's nothing you could do."

Marc gazed at her for a few seconds in silence. He reached out and gently brushed a loose lock of hair from her forehead and saw the faint scar on her brow, as though it had been burned in. A rush of protective anger hit him. He wouldn't let Samantha be taken the way Talitha was. So, this was the one he needed to save as Talitha had said.

"Oh, Samantha!" he whispered, and stooping, he kissed the scar as the girl burst into tears.

XV

Cinderella

"Konstan, I'm not going!" Samantha said for the umpteenth time, getting up and slapping her folder on the desk. She turned to face him. They were in her sitting room, trying to get in a little relaxation after the hectic morning. Konstan, who was lounging on the couch, sat up.

"Look, my dear *sisia*, why can't you be yourself as I used to know you? At the Academy, you used to be a normal girl who could wear a pretty dress and be happy about it. You could use the time off!" he urged her.

"You sound like everyone else," Samantha replied, frustrated. "I've had plenty of time off since Aiyra arrived."

"It still doesn't add up to the amount of free time I've had over two years," Konstan pointed out. "And you've been under a lot of stress. *And*, if I heard you correctly, you were going to discuss your knowledge of the Marauders in more depth with the Captain so that you could both figure out a way to help Aiyra with her trauma." Samantha stopped short and slapped her forehead.

"How could I forget?" she moaned. "Oh, alright, alright, I'll go!"

"Good!" Konstan said with satisfaction, jumping up from the couch. "I'll take care of anything left on your schedule, sis. You start getting ready. The party starts around five thirty," he reminded her. He ducked out.

Passing the technicians' work room, he happened to see that Marc was just leaving after making sure that every file had successfully made it back into the data banks. He ran after him.

"Captain!" he called.

Marc stopped and looked back. "Hey there! I bet you've been busy. What are you up to?"

"Uh, well – I'm not working right now. See, I want Samantha to attend the celebration tonight. She's worried about attending. . . I think she told you why. I talked her into it, though, and I was wondering if you'd mind keeping an eye on her since I'll be taking over her schedule."

Marc tried not to laugh at the youth's innocent expression. "Don't worry, Konstan," he assured him with a straight face. "I'll look after her if she needs anything. However, when your shift is over, I think you should try and come down for a little while. . . Aiyra would like that." Konstan reddened a bit, seeing the mischievous look in the captain's eyes.

"I suppose she would! She didn't get much of a birthday. I'll try, sir." Amused, Marc watched the suddenly-not-so-confident engineer rush off.

"Highly suspicious," he laughed to himself, and went on his way.

~~~

Samantha stepped in front of her mirror and surveyed herself, gently tugging on the clip earrings Konstan had given her for her birthday a few years before. It was almost five o'clock now, and the sun was preparing to sink into the sea. Konstan, who had only a few tasks left, was waiting to see his friend off.

"Is it alright?" Samantha asked anxiously. Her hair was swept up in soft waves, crowned with loops of pearls and silver flowers. The gown of icy lilac silk shantung was in a traditional Almedran style. The bodice sparkled with loops of seed beads framing diamond-shaped crystals, and a moderate illusion neckline dotted with gems faded into a beaded choker. Puffed cap sleeves were hung with many tiers of beads, looped over the cascading Grecian sleeves, and the skirt fell in sweeping folds which just brushed the ground. A matching over dress was pinned to the back at the shoulders and wrapped around in front, forming a moderate train trimmed in frothy lace. Konstan took one look at her and had to laugh.

"Are you kidding? You look like a princess. Come on now, I still have some work to do and the captain wants me down at the party later. Let's get you going."

Samantha hesitated. "Can't I wait until you're ready?" The answer to this was a shove out the door.

~~~

Laughter mingled with the bouncing tune of flutes, violins, and exotic instruments as Marc wended his way through the crowded pavilion, Aiyra in tow. The sun was setting, painting the sky apricot, peach, and coral, and creating a sparkling path on the bay. Colorful lights bejeweled the trees, reflecting in the dancing fountains as men and women swirled around the gardens to the tune of an unfamiliar waltz. Eventually Marc made it to the steps at the far end of the pavilion, where the governor's table was set under a bright canopy.

"Ah, Captain Hesslin!" the governor boomed over the music. "Good to see you!" He came down the steps and shook Marc's hand.

"Good evening, Governor Ventiin," Marc returned.

"And here's little Aiyra," Ventiin added, turning to the girl and gently taking her hand. "I heard yesterday was your birthday! Consider this your very own celebration as well," he told her. Aiyra thanked him politely. The governor turned back to Marc.

"Captain, I've been told that you played a pivotal role in the Battle of Maltara," he began.

Here we go again, Marc groaned inwardly. Aiyra started laughing for no reason and hastily turned to watch the dancers. Her eyes widened as she saw a way of saving her father from the conversation.

"A'da!" she said excitedly. Marc glanced over. Others were turning their heads to look at the young woman in glittering array who stood uncertainly at the top of the wide garden stairs. Marc did a double-take. If he had thought that the pink gown was a nice change from green, then this was the only real-life Cinderella he had ever seen.

"Samantha!" he said under his breath. He brightened, realizing his opportunity for escape.

"Excuse me, Governor," he apologized with a slight bow. He descended into the pavilion and made his way through the crowd again. He found Samantha waiting hesitantly and surveying the crowd. Her eyes lit up with relief when she saw him standing there, and she gratefully took the arm he offered her.

"You look nice," Marc said respectfully, steering her through the crowd.

"Thank you. . ." Samantha murmured.

"Is Konstan with you?"

"No, he's still working. I was going to wait for him, but-" Samantha half-shrugged, shaking a loose curl out of her eyes.

"I see," Marc replied as they arrived at the governor's table. Ventiin arose from his seat when he saw Samantha.

"And who is this young lady?" he asked Marc reproachfully. "Didn't you invite her to the ceremony yesterday, captain?" He shook his head with laughing disapproval and smiled at Samantha.

"Sir, this is Ms. Anselle, one of the *Lumenara's* top engineers," Marc replied, flushing a little. "Her brother is still on duty, so she's with me for a while." Samantha recalled how to curtsy and murmured a greeting, pleased that Marc had made no worse introduction.

"An engineer! I would have thought you were a princess," Ventiin teased her gently. Samantha laughed a little.

"Peasants are as the nobility among my people," she admitted. "We all have a soul, a body, a family, a cross, and a life; and royal clothing doesn't take much but the crystals found in the earth and the silk of the spider."

"A wise way of doing things," Ventiin observed. "You're a sweet girl, Ms. Anselle. Now, I'll let you two run along to dance. Go on!" he gave the pair a push as they protested, and they soon found themselves trapped on the dance floor.

Marc looked helplessly at Samantha. He could tell that Ventiin was not about to let them get away without at least one dance. Possibly because he had heard the rumor of the captain and his daughter and the mysterious mother no one had known of, and suspected a tragedy; or perhaps it was because Samantha was so lovely, Aiyra so sweet, and Marc so lonely. Samantha fixed her eyes on the dancers, trying to pretend she didn't understand their predicament.

The merry piping of the flutes became a sweet-toned, gentle waltz and Samantha found herself forgetting the stress that weighed on her shoulders. Her face cleared and she realized that Marc was feeling just as awkward as she was. She turned and looked at him.

"Do you think we should?" she asked, holding out her hands. "He's waiting, and I have a feeling he won't let us alone until we do." Marc took her hands and then stopped, looking into her face.

"I'm afraid to," he said, almost ashamed. "You're so beautiful that I'm beginning to think I don't really know who you are, Samantha. Is this you, or are you really just the professional young woman who's just as afraid of her past as I am of mine?" Samantha hesitated as they instinctively began to spin to the melody being played.

"People change over the years," she said. "Konstan told me to be more like myself. . . but I'm afraid I'm being more like my old self than my real self."

"Yes, time changes people," Marc granted. "But this must be part of you, Samantha. Just as your professional side is a part of you. Perhaps you don't know the real you, either. Everyone quotes the old saying, 'be true to yourself,' but how *can* you be if you don't know yourself?"

Samantha shook her head. "I don't know anything anymore," she confessed. "I don't know who I am, Marc. Am I a girl slated to wed a Marauder king? One who is tied down by the world? Am I just an engineer? Or am I a normal girl who can find a normal way through life?'"

"Probably the latter," Marc murmured thoughtfully. He looked down at her hands, so small in his. "Maybe, Samantha, don't be afraid to be a woman. You are afraid to love and to be loved, so you've trained yourself to hide in your profession and your work. It *is* a beautiful part of you, Samantha, but not half as beautiful as your whole self." He looked earnestly into her eyes.

"If you can trust me, as you said you could, believe me when I say that I won't let Medrhos find you. Besides, how *could* he find you? Among thousands of years and billions of people and trillions of stars and planets, you are impossible for him to reach. And you could not have found a safer place to be than the *Lumenara;* you know from my past how much they fear me."

Samantha smiled then and moved her hand to his shoulder. "Riddle me this," she said. "Why do you make perfect sense to me when I don't to myself?"

Marc just laughed and swung her around as the music cascaded to an end. A young man leapt up on the stage and called for a member of the audience, any foreigner, to share a song from their homeland. Samantha's eyes sparkled and she took her chance. She was helped up to the stage, where she stood and sang of her home, and the silken thread that bound God and man, life and love, time, and eternity.

Marc was fascinated until he noticed the maiden growing distracted during the third stanza. He followed her gaze to a certain man in the audience, who was plucking roses and tossing them at the foot of the stage in between overly flattering remarks. Marc looked around for a projectile of his own. He found a rather solid wild berry cupcake on a nearby table of refreshments and, taking careful aim, made his mark.

The muffin squarely struck the young man's overfilled glass of lemonade, which splashed over his perfect garments and jerked him to his feet with a yelp. Marc choked on a laugh and turned back before he could be noticed. Samantha's eyes were laughing and she lightly tripped over a few words as she struggled to keep a straight face. She made it through to the end, however, and descended the stage amid applause. Marc was there to draw her safely through the crowd.

"You have a beautiful voice," he complimented her. They began making their way back towards the governor's table.

"Thank you," Samantha said shyly. "And thank you for knocking 'Sir Distraction's' glass over when you did!"

Marc laughed. "It was a pleasure! He was ruining your song."

"And a minute before that, he was making faces," Samantha shook her head. "There always seems to be that one person in the audience." She shook down her hair and untied the train of her dress.

"Perhaps that's one good reason for looking more like myself!" she added, looking much more like the engineer Marc knew. Aiyra danced up to them, Konstan in tow once more.

"Much better, sis!" His eyes twinkled as though he had planned Samantha's rediscovery of self. "I haven't heard you sing in forever!" he remarked, giving her a squeeze. "And yes, I was just in time to see you knock out that guy, Captain. Couldn't have done it better myself!"

"I was just taking a page out of your own book," Marc teased, ruffling the boy's hair. "Have you eaten? No? Well, what boy can survive on an empty stomach? Aiyra hasn't been eating much, so please set her a good example," he called over his shoulder, drawing Samantha away.

Konstan watched them for a second and then headed for the nearest table. Aiyra followed, suddenly subdued as though she somehow had nothing to say. Konstan soon began to feel the silence and glanced over his shoulder to see his friend watching him. He stopped.

"Is something wrong?" he inquired. Aiyra hesitated, began to shake her head, but stopped. The wind ruffled her loose curls and Konstan abruptly noticed the dancing lights and stars reflected in those eyes, so mirrored in the variegated surroundings of the night that they could not choose any single color to reflect.

"I just like being with you," the girl said frankly.

"I like being with you, too! It's nice having a little sister." When the girl just looked down and did not reply, he had an inkling that there was something else on her mind.

"Aiyra, if you need to talk, I'm always here to listen," he reminded her, setting aside his plate and hers.

"I am afraid. . ."

"Of what?"

"That something will happen to you." Aiyra raised her head. "I used to know you, Konstan, though I did not remember it, and was not sure, until last night. I met you before my mother died. Here, where we are standing now. And you were with me for several years, before we were separated." She studied his puzzled expression. "Konstan, if anything happens to you—"

"Nothing will happen to me that isn't for the best, Aiyra. Don't worry so! Even if something did happen to me, you'll have those who are closest to you: your father and Samantha."

"Not you?" she asked, astonished.

"Well, I – didn't wish to assume so."

Aiyra held out her hand to him. The youth took it, a trifle bewildered, and Aiyra drew him into the crowd of dancers. Lifting his hand, she shyly placed her own against it. "Please teach me, big brother?"

Konstan's eyes softened as he looked down at her sweet face.

"I'll teach you, and I'll always be here for you, little princess. Don't be frightened anymore, not for yourself or for me. Everything is going to be alright now that you're here with us, safe and sound. I'll never let you have to go back to the Marauders, even if that takes me to the time you first knew me."

Aiyra looked up at him, lips trembling, but she smiled as though he made her feel safe, and hugged him because the music had stopped. Konstan gave her a squeeze and then with smiling eyes, pulled her along as a waltz started.

They whirled in circles around the dancing fountain, finding again that Aiyra's perfect grace melded with his skill until they forgot all else. Swirling gowns shimmered in the light and footsteps fell rhythmically to the music. All was lovely until Aiyra stumbled to a stop with a gasp. Her hand flew to her head.

"Aiyra! What is it?"

"Just a headache – can we leave the crowd?" she panted with a quick smile. Konstan put his arm around her and guided her to a quiet garden alcove with a view of the party below; and Aiyra leaned her head on her friend's shoulder as the stars began to dance overhead.

"Just never get hurt, Konstan," she whispered. "Please, never."

XVI

Pearl

"But how did you know that there was a battle station nearby?" Ventiin asked, intent on getting Marc to relate every detail off the battle.

Experience, Marc longed to say, and be done with it. Instead, he patiently explained that the size of type C Marauder ships and their primitive fuel could only last a few hours, and thus a swarm of C ships meant they had a base nearby. Taking out that base crippled the fleet and allowed the decimated Vestar forces to gain the upper hand.

Meanwhile, Samantha was conversing nearby with a few women who wanted to know the details of her costume, a teen who hoped to be an engineer, and a man who knew the 'entire' history of Almedra.

Tradition, experience and practice, and you've got a lot to learn, she tried not to exclaim, as the women tried to offer suggestions for 'upgrading' her dress. The youth tried to lobby for a position on the *Lumenara*, and the historical know-it-all tried to insist that 'Anselle' meant 'of royal birth' when all it meant was 'silver web', coming from her ancestors' occupation as silk weavers. Samantha suppressed a laugh and patiently explained the history behind every detail of her outfit, gave the boy advice on how to practice for his profession, sent him to Marc, and corrected the man's Almedran vocabulary.

At last, she had a few moments of peace and she watched the dancers sway. Someone tapped her shoulder. She thought it would be Marc, but before she could turn around, she was swept into the crowd. Bewildered, she looked up to see that it was 'Sir Distraction' who was waltzing with her. She pulled away.

"Excuse me, but please ask first, *then* dance," she corrected him, freeing her hands.

"Forgive me; I was afraid someone else would dance with you first. Allow me to introduce myself: I am Rad Ventiin." He waited as though that meant as much as a plethora of roses in a crystal vase.

"Um. . . the governor's son, I assume," Samantha guessed, seeing that he wanted an answer. Rad looked pleased.

"You're a smart girl! What do you know of me? I assume Father has told you *something* about me."

"Absolutely nothing, actually," Samantha sighed, looking for Marc. Rad mistook the sigh as one of regret and instantly softened. He pulled her arm through his, much to her annoyance, and tugged her out of the pavilion and into a secluded garden. Seating her on a bench, and gently preventing her from leaving, he began to share his life story, his talents, and his achievements. . .

Samantha struggled not to fall asleep and restrained herself from shoving him into the nearest rosebush. He did remind her strangely of Medrhos before she had known who he was. He, too, was lonely and arrogant, adventurous, overly daring, and thought too highly of himself, Samantha noted.

His 'achievements' included nearly drowning, hunting and killing an entire pack of wolves on his own, and capturing several trespassing vessels single-handedly while almost blowing up the city. Supposedly he was the commander of the Maedrian fleet, but

Samantha wasn't sure how. From what she could tell, he was no one that anyone should follow – anyone in their right mind, at least.

But his baby sister had died, his fiancé had been murdered, and his best friend, a fellow member of the fleet, was shot down on a mission and drowned in the bay. It seemed that his daring and arrogance had been caused by guilt stemming from an unrealistic belief that he was responsible for those tragedies. Samantha exhaled and tried to find something to say that might help him (and, incidentally, free her from being stuck with him).

"Commander-"

"Rad," he corrected her.

"Rad. I think your problem is that you think you are responsible in some way for all those deaths. That feeling comes to even the most cautious of us. It's unrealistic, and you know none of them would want you to feel or respond in this way," she pointed out. "It's affecting your whole life, Rad. Sometimes it is hard to accept our innocence in some things. Relax; you're fine."

Rad stared at her. He blinked. Grabbing her hand, he pulled her back to the pavilion and up to his father, who was sitting on the edge of the fountain with his niece.

"Father! I'm going to marry this woman," Rad announced, drawing a few amazed looks from those nearby.

Samantha's jaw dropped. There was an awkward silence as Ventiin looked to see what she would do. An idea came to mind as Samantha listened to the trickling of the fountain. The engineer shut her mouth with a little smirk, and drove the heel of her boot into the back of Rad's knee. He fell headfirst into the pool. Thankfully he didn't hit his head in doing so.

"I'll thank you *again* to *ask* first!" she said dryly. Ventiin looked at his spluttering son and burst out laughing.

"He needed that," he said, turning to Samantha. "He's not the hero he thinks he is. Don't mind him, dear." He looked behind her. "And here's your true hero."

Samantha glanced back and saw Marc standing there, his brow creased as he looked anxiously from Rad to Samantha. When he saw that she was hardly disturbed by Rad's behavior, his eyes twinkled and he offered her a high five. Samantha caught his hand instead and taught him a dance that was like a wedding between a minuet and the mazurka. Aiyra, no longer feeling the headache for the time being, was dancing a Cythian gavotte with a young girl while Konstan guarded her plate from a hungry puppy. Everything spun past in a swirl of pastel rainbows, while the moon climbed higher to shed its light more brightly on the couples below.

Smiling, Marc drew Samantha aside and they walked down to the beach. The dark cliff faces looked almost friendly at night as the pair crossed the sand and stood at the water's edge. Marc picked up a sparkling shell and pried it open. A tiny pearl lay nestled inside, not unlike the seed pearls on Aiyra's ring.

"Talitha must have collected almost a hundred of these just for one ring," he murmured. Samantha looked over his shoulder.

"Aiyra's?" Marc nodded. He flung the shell away and placed the pearl in Samantha's hand, where it lay like a little silver moon. The captain did a double-take when he saw a silver flash on Samantha's wrist. It curved along her arms and glinted beneath the high collar of her gown.

"Moon scars!" Samantha said, noticing his expression. "It's common among my people. The old legends say that the Almedran moon, Photar, was the source of the spider's thread. Moonbeams falling to earth were gathered by the creatures and woven, strung across branches and fences for us to gather every morning. Every Almedran's life was built around, and depended on silk; it kept our world economically stable and safe, and we found many life-saving methods of using the silk."

"At last we realized God's presence in nature; that its actions are from Him. But the one thing missing in our lives was patience, so He gave us a reminder of the spider's patience and industry. It's for perseverance, too, for a spider will rebuild her web no matter how many times it is broken." She looked down at the silver lines that traced along her arms. "It usually shows when there is a flower moon or a harvest moon; but that depends on the planet."

"But that's the legend's story," Marc replied. "What really caused it? Do you know? Or is it natural?"

"It's natural," she replied. "That is, it depends on genetics. As to why we have it, I don't know; all I know is that it often shows on my hands no matter what moon it is-"

"And that's why you wear gloves so often!" Marc interjected.

Samantha nodded and finished, "And that when I either have nearly forgotten God's presence and need a reminder of Him or of strength; or when I know I've done right."

"Which is it now?" Marc asked. "The type of moon, forgetfulness, or good actions?"

Samantha smiled and rubbed her arms. "I think He's happy with me for not arguing with Him about you."

"Really, you've been arguing about me behind my back?" he teased. "Just for that-" He put his hand in the shallow water and splashed her. She shrieked, laughed, and ran, after causing him to stumble backwards into the water. Marc chased her and they ran up and down the shoreline until they were breathless with laughter. They flopped down on the sand.

"Oh, look!" Samantha gasped a moment later. The water was beginning to glow and sparkle with an aqua light. It began in patches until it spread along the beach and far out into the bay, even lighting the remains of the church tower all covered with flowers. Samantha couldn't resist; she kicked off her shoes and stepped in. The water was warm now, and the glow caught on the hem of her skirts as though it were beaded with turquoise.

"It must be phosphorescence from the crystals in the sunken mines," Marc guessed, coming over and studying a handful of the seawater. "The radioactive ingredient must have been such that it died after a few decades or so of saltwater, and three hundred years' time has eroded the crystals. They must coat the seabed now," he observed. He looked out at the tower.

"I have an idea!" he said suddenly. "Let's take one of those water speeders out; we'll be able to see the ocean ruins quite clearly now."

Samantha agreed to this plan, and soon they were out on the water, following the waves. Marc brought the craft down on the water's surface and let it drift. Below lay the tell-tale white stones and scattered bricks. Looking down, Samantha could almost see the city again as it had been, beautiful and ancient, but weary and sad, with tyrants, noblemen, peasants, and slaves.

"It's strange to think that Aiyra once lived, worked, walked down there!" she whispered.

"Yes. . . and in a sense, still is," Marc muttered.

"*Was*, Captain. That was in the past; she's here with us now, free and safe. Let's not open Pandora's box again by considering all of time to be accessible when it is not God's Will. We all have to think that way, for the sake of preserving whatever sanity we possess," she said with a little laugh.

Marc concurred and took the wheel again, wondering what every day had been like for his wife and daughter, every pain, every shadow of a smile, every instant of labor.

"I'd like to see the church tower Konstan and Aiyra told us about," Samantha requested, pointing it out in the distance. "I'll pick some of the sea-lavender and lilies for her."

The craft skipped lightly over the water again, and Marc brought it as close to the tower as he could, the nose of the speeder bumping against the rock. Many of the rosy blossoms had closed for the night, but the white bay lilies and the lavender flowers weren't quite sleeping. Samantha leaned out to gather the blossoms and glanced down into the lit water just as Aiyra had done; but a wave rocked the boat and she lost her balance.

"Oh!"

Down she went and the water closed over her head. It was a strange feeling, like swimming in an illumined hotel pool on a summer night, but there was no solid surface beneath her feet. Although her drenched gown was decidedly not buoyant, Samantha neglected to panic. There was an ancient façade across the way, and its shadowy doorways might have been home to merchant's shops, weaver's homes, or bakeries. A crumbled fountain and a broken pillar told tales of ancient conversations at the well, and military ceremonies held around the eroded monument to an age-old king.

The waves swirled seagreen, and for a split-second Samantha felt a chill stab her as she thought she saw swirling figures in doorways, in streets, the church and the gardens and the halls – Samantha almost shrieked aloud and realized that she was in the middle of drowning. The next moment found her dumped in a heap in the bottom of the water speeder. Marc struck her back as she spit out water.

"Take it easy! Get all that water out of your lungs."

"Couldn't you have pulled me out a little quicker so I wouldn't have to?" Samantha choked. Marc looked confused.

"Quicker? You were only in for as long as it took me to lean over the side of the speeder and grab you."

Samantha rubbed her head. "Oh." They both caught their breath and let their adrenalized hearts relax.

"I'm so sorry, Samantha!" Marc said at last. "I missed the memo on taking an unexpected swim. It must be the new fashion! I hear everyone's doing it. Wait, here we go – I'll do it myself."

He slid in backwards with a splash that soaked Samantha again. The engineer burst out laughing and splashed him back. Marc just grinned and rested his arms on the side of the speeder.

"Samantha, thank you for saying what you did about time," he remarked. "It reminded me of what Talitha said. . . that she's not the one who needs me most. I thought she meant Aiyra; but Samantha, it's you. And because of you, Samantha, I'm no longer tempted to break God's rules and bring her back." He looked at her fondly. Samantha blushed and couldn't think of anything to say in reply.

"Er, captain, weren't we to discuss how we might help Aiyra?" she asked quickly.

"Argh!" said Marc, slapping his forehead. He winced as he splashed saltwater into his eyes, much to Samantha's concerned amusement.

"With all the problems on the ship today, I didn't get a chance to talk with Aiyra. She was going to tell me about something before she fell asleep last night. But why has she been hiding it?"

"She told me she didn't want to worry you. At least, when it comes to the physical problems she's been having."

"Which are what?" Marc demanded. Samantha briefly mentioned the headaches and nerve pain that she had known of.

"As for whatever else she might be hiding, I don't know what it is or why she's not telling you," Samantha sighed.

"Well, the surest way to find out is to let her know that we're here to help her heal, not to keep ourselves from getting hurt," Marc murmured. "She needs to not be afraid of worrying us."

"Using the royal plural?" the engineer teased.

"Of course not! I mean you and I, silly," he retorted.

"Oh, so suddenly it's not 'worrying *all* of us', you, Konstan, Truitt and me; it's just you and me."

"Well. . . we kind of get stuck together most of the time," Marc answered defensively. "And we're the ones discussing the problem, so it makes sense-" he stopped when he realized that Samantha was biting back a smile.

"In other words," she prompted.

"Uh, in other words, I consider you to be my best friend."

"Mm, in other words you've already forgotten that you've already said what you're trying to say. You'd best get in, captain," she returned. "I think I saw a shark down there."

"Sharks? We strongly disapprove of sharks right now," Marc joked. He climbed in and sat next to her. "I just realized that I probably shouldn't have done that."

"What, climb in? Did you want to get eaten? I haven't seen a shark's menu, but you're probably on it. For all I know he's looking for a burger for his date. Probably even has sea roses and luminescent crystals on a table for two."

Marc laughed at her. "No, my watch," he explained, examining it. "The last waterproof item I bought lasted two seconds flat after being in the rain." He turned to her with a smile. Reaching over, he pushed back her hair and gently signed her scarred forehead with the cross.

"And yes, I know what you wanted me to say," he whispered. A scratching beep made them both jump.

"I guess there's your answer about the watch!" Samantha exclaimed, hugging herself. The breeze made the warm water feel cold on her skin. Konstan's voice came over the speaker.

"Captain?"

"Marc here – go ahead, Konstan." There was an instant's pause as they heard the boy draw a shaky breath.

"Come back to the ship. It's Aiyra – she's been hiding more than we thought."

XVII

Menace

"Aiyra?" Marc flung open the door to the ICU. There, among the flashing lights, life support systems, and scanners, lay his daughter. Marc stooped and gathered her into his arms.

"Aiyra, baby, what's wrong?" he breathed, feeling how violently she shook.

"I am sorry, A'da!" she whispered. She pulled his hands to her cheek and clung to him. "I – should have told you!"

"Hush, dear, it's alright," Marc soothed her. "I'm here now. Doctor, what's wrong with her?"

"It's an implant given her by one of her former 'owners,'" Elise replied, stepping over. "It was deactivated when she left that system, but it seems that something has caused it to reactivate. It's trying to reestablish its connection with her neural network, but in doing so it's damaging her nervous system."

Marc looked down at his daughter, whose tanned skin was almost white, her hair drenched with sweat, and her breath was coming in gasps. He moaned softly and held her close.

"What . . . was it for?"

"The civilization of the Keltars was highly advanced, although its computers were not up to our standards," Konstan answered, leaving his place at the computer. "Everything was controlled by machinery. . . *everything*."

"Everything?" Marc repeated, his heart sinking. Elise and Konstan nodded.

"The implant allowed Aiyra to utilize the machinery necessary for her work – doors and kitchens included," Konstan sighed. "Nothing moved unless it was needed at that very moment. But not only was the implant for 'practical purposes,' but it could also be used to subdue or punish slaves."

Marc cringed and looked down at his daughter. She silently confirmed this, and Marc finally understood. Aiyra's trauma, her reluctance to tell anyone when she was hurting, her fear of crowds and civilization, her sudden changes in character – she had been trained. And the implant –

"Is likely the source of all the computer incidents lately," Konstan said, reading Marc's expression. "Ever since she reached the *Lumenara,* it's started to function again. It's possible that she subconsciously reactivated it when she realized she would have to deal with explaining it; or that something on the right frequency caused it to try and regain access to her neural network."

Looking down, Konstan covered Aiyra's hand with his. Samantha spoke up then. She had been studying the rather blurred image of the implant on the screen.

"Is it possible," she asked Konstan, "that our technology, and the various electronic signals and frequencies which we use today, are the same as those which the Keltar used?"

"I have a bad feeling that you're right," he replied. "As soon as Aiyra told me of it, I did a little research. . . from what I could see, the Keltar, although decimated by disease five hundred years ago, reestablished a civilization when the survivors married into the Aithon peoples of Aquila in the great Galaxy."

"The Aithonians!" Marc exclaimed. "They were the ones who developed our technology a century ago–"

"Likely aided by the knowledge of the Keltars," Elise finished. There were a few moments of silence broken only by a despairing whimper from Aiyra.

"Angel, what's wrong? Does it hurt worse?" Marc asked anxiously. The girl shook her head.

"No, not worse," she moaned. "But I won't be able to control it now–"

"No, Aiyra!" Konstan comforted her. "We're going to remove it so that you won't have to worry about anything."

"Captain!" Dr. Menendez said gently, laying her hand on Marc's arm. "Let her be still now, please. I must take another scan. Then Samantha and Konstan will be able to tell us how best to deactivate and remove the implant."

"No, please!" Aiyra begged. "Do not scan it again!"

"Aiyra, honey, I know it hurts," the doctor replied, leaning over her and gently touching her face. "But we have to get a full scan of the implant so we can study it."

"It's okay, baby, I'll stay right here." Marc held her hands as Elise set the scanners at either side of Aiyra's head.

"Lie still," the doctor warned. She left to set the program again. A green light flashed on each side of the scanner. Aiyra gasped and struggled to remain still as her father tried to distract her. Samantha grabbed Konstan's shoulder and prevented him from running to his friend's side.

"Konstan, the more we concentrate, the sooner we can help her!" she promised. Elise began the scan, taking screenshots of every angle. Marc looked up and saw the evil, yet surprisingly small steel implant located just an inch or so above her right ear.

"A'da!" Aiyra pleaded. Her breath was coming quickly, and it seemed to them that the scan was disrupting the implant so that it pained Aiyra even more.

"Almost!" Elise answered, rather pale herself.

"Hang on!" Marc encouraged his daughter, silently about to panic.

"Hurry!" Samantha said under her breath.

"I think I can fix it!" Konstan cried, about to snap.

Whirling, he pulled a small, strongly magnetized screwdriver from his belt. Glancing back at the screen, he carefully drew the tip of the screwdriver along Aiyra's temple. Marc and Samantha looked at the screen and saw a small metal disk jiggle, and then turn –

Aiyra snapped upright and vomited. The color quickly returning to her face, her trembling ceased. Presently she rubbed her head and looked around. She saw her father's tousled, damp hair and missing coat, then Samantha's tangled curls and soaked gown.

"Did everyone decide to go for a swim after we left?" she asked quizzically. "I thought the skies were clear." Marc choked on a laugh of relief and tugged lightly on her curls.

"Samantha here thought it was a nice night for falling into the ocean and almost drowning!" he replied. "So, I figured it must be the new fashion."

"Well, 'superman' here thought I should do some underwater sightseeing so he gave me a few seconds to drown," Samantha shot back, playfully pushing Marc aside and kissing Aiyra's head. Aiyra turned to Konstan.

"I'm hungry. Konstan, why did you not feed me like A'da told you to?" Konstan shook his head at her, laughing.

"I'll feed you, I promise! It's probably a good thing I didn't, though!" he said ruefully. "You *did* get sick."

"Nothing but liquids for you tonight, young lady," Elise said sternly. "You've had a lot of damage done to your nervous system, not to mention your neural network. There's no telling just how much damage or how long it will take to heal. If you had let me scan it, silly –" Aiyra winced and shamefacedly leaned her head on Marc's arm.

"You don't have to be afraid to hid things from us, dear," he said softly. "We're here to help you, not to avoid worrying about you." Aiyra nodded.

"And Konstan," Elise continued, "I think you'd agree with me that the implant isn't permanently shut down. Something could reactivate it, so we'll need you to rest, Aiyra, while we study the x-rays." Konstan agreed.

"Which means," Marc added, "that the two of you – Konstan and Samantha – will only be on duty half the workday. You'll need assistants. Tell Truitt to begin training a few more engineers."

Samantha had to smile, thinking of the one willing recruit who was probably fast asleep after his 'exciting conversation with a real engineer.' Everyone stopped again to look at Aiyra.

"You need to sleep, dear," Marc said tenderly.

"She needs to eat something," Konstan added sheepishly.

"I think she needs to get away from that scanner," Samantha said dryly, shutting it off as she noted the still-blinking lights and Aiyra's still-pained expression.

"I think she needs to do all three," Elise replied, nodding her thanks. "Now go on, all of you! It's past midnight, and all decent people have been in bed for a few hours. All doctors should be finishing their morning coffee," she joked. "And get out of those wet clothes before you catch a cold!" She shooed them out of the ICU as she put out the lights, one by one.

XVIII

Competence

Morning found the four seated around a table near the garden fountains, drinking their coffee and wondering how raspberry, dark chocolate, and cream cheese pie could count as breakfast. They had to agree that it didn't quite make it, and hastily added an extra round of bacon, buttered toast, and blueberries. This decision might have been due to the richness of the pseudo-breakfast food; then again, it might have been made because they saw Elise heading their way.

"Good morning!" she said, and sat down with them.

"What's that?" asked Konstan, nodding to the glass of suspiciously un-coffeelike liquid she held.

"What, this? I officially finished my morning coffee at precisely 3:00 this morning," she smiled. "This is my 'tis almost lunchtime' tea."

"Betrayal!" Marc joked. "How dare you join us for coffee and have tea instead!"

"Coffee," Samantha declared, "is the best drink in the galaxy. Er, two galaxies. No hyperbole intended." She looked at Aiyra, who nodded in agreement, her first cup of coffee ever now almost empty.

"Hyperbole is the worst thing in the universe," Konstan explained. Aiyra choked on her coffee and flung a piece of bacon at him. Konstan looked at the bacon in his glass.

"Mm, bacon coffee! Bacon makes everything better."

"Everything? Or is that hyperbole?" Aiyra guessed.

"Well, *almost* everything," Konstan laughed, munching on his toast. "Maybe it wouldn't improve the flavor of insects. And shrimp." Aiyra made a disgusted face and dumped her toast onto his plate. The boy hastily promised not to mention insects again.

"Seriously, though, I can relate," Samantha said, turning to Elise again. "I've had nights where I sat up drinking coffee from midnight until five a.m. It *is* possible to get a little tired of coffee after that."

"Quite! Cheers!" Elise raised her glass.

"To what?" asked Konstan, still thinking about bacon.

"How about, to getting that implant fixed?" Marc replied.

"I'll drink to that," Konstan sighed, and everyone reached for their coffee. Aiyra's hand fell limply on the table. She sat still for a second, trying to get her arm to cooperate.

"Oh," she groaned softly.

"The muscles aren't responding?" Elise asked. Aiyra nodded. She tried to lean her now aching head and jammed neck on her hand, but she couldn't accomplish that, either. Elise got up and pressed lightly on the palm of Aiyra's hand.

"Do you feel that?"

"A little."

"Then it's not truly paralyzed," she said. "I'm not sure why it would have happened now, and not before; but can you stand?" Aiyra stood.

"It seems to be just my arms," she observed. "And my neck, as well."

"Alright then, we'll get you down to the infirmary and try something. Acupuncture may help-"

"Ouch," Samantha muttered.

"Alternatively, physical therapy," the doctor finished, giving Samantha a look. "Come on, dear." She took Aiyra's arm as Marc received a call from the Vestar Fleet commander. The ringtone crackled and he got up.

"I'll have to get rid of this thing soon," he muttered. He turned to Elise. "I'll try to make this quick. Aiyra, I'll be down soon to take care of you, honey." He ran for the elevators.

"Well, I'll come-" Konstan began, but jumped when his phone rang wildly.

"Konstan, get down here!" Truitt barked. "I have a bunch of would-be-engineer kids tearing up the wiring!" Konstan winced and shot an apologetic look at Aiyra.

"Well, at least I-" Samantha began.

"And you can tell Samantha to get down here, too! I've got a so-called engineer with a crush on her, and he's trying to fix our perfect computers to impress her!" Truitt snapped.

"Ouch!" Konstan and Samantha both winced.

"Sorry, sweetheart! I'll get back as soon as I can," Samantha promised, and dashed off with Konstan. Aiyra stared for a second, wondering what had just happened.

"Come on, dear," Elise laughed. "Doctors are reliable, anyway. I'll take care of you." She led the way to the infirmary.

~~~

"Sir, what do you mean that I have to leave the system?" Marc asked, bewildered. The image of Commander Flynn of the Vestar Fleet flickered on the screen.

"Captain, the *Delta IV* has returned with another three thousand refugees," Flynn repeated patiently. "I want you, and you specifically, to rendezvous with the *Delta* and relieve her of her passengers."

"But the *Lumenara* can't even take that many!" Marc protested.

"I know – I'll have the *Indelible* take 1,500 of the refugees on board before she leaves for the great Galaxy," Flynn explained. "The rendezvous will take place in the system of Soltarra, on Wednesday at precisely 0900 hours."

"Sir-" Marc stammered for a minute, wondering how to explain his loathing to leave Maedra.

"Marc. . . what is it?"

Marc hung his head for a moment and studied the pen in his hand.

"My wife. . . is buried here. She was murdered three hundred years ago in Maedrean time. I just don't want to leave-" He looked up and saw that Flynn understood.

"Marc, as soon as you have completed this mission, I'll leave you free to return to Maedra for as long as you like. You've worked tirelessly for the past two years, more than any other captain of my fleet. You deserve a long rest," he said kindly. Marc exhaled and nodded.

"I'll leave soon," he promised. "But my daughter needs medical attention; it may be best if I left her here."

Flynn smiled. "I understand. You may leave anytime between now and 1400 hours tomorrow, and still arrive on time."

Marc gave his thanks and reached to snap off the video. "I just hope she'll be alright," he muttered, wondering what would happen next.

~~~

Konstan and Samantha ducked as a wave of sparks shot across the room.

"Truitt!" Konstan yelled above the noise as young engineer enthusiasts alternately shrieked at the mistake of one, then clamored for a job. "*Truitt!*"

The man appeared, coughing, and impatiently waved away the kids who tried to schedule an immediate appointment.

"There you are!" he called, seeing the pair. "Come on, that idiot tried to fix the situation with the coolant and cut half the wires to the engine. If we don't get it fixed now, we won't be going anywhere anytime soon." Konstan darted after him, Samantha on his heels. A hand grabbed her wrist.

"Ms. Anselle!" the boy said, delighted. Samantha groaned, seeing he was the same one from the party. "Show me how I can help!"

"Do you *really* want to help?" Samantha asked impatiently. The boy nodded. "Then first, let go of my hand, and then round up your friends and get them outside so they don't add to the problem." He ran off and Samantha shook her hair out of her eyes, wondering what disaster the engineering world would come to.

"Samantha, stop daydreaming!" Truitt shouted. The sprinkler system was going off again and steam was filling the room.

"Coming!"

Samantha joined them. As Konstan snapped off the power in each circuit, Samantha swiftly replaced each of the snipped wires, while Truitt busied himself overriding the smoke detectors.

Suddenly something blew in the machinery and the humming of the generators wound down with a deflated whir.

"My ship!" Truitt groaned, and watched in dismay as the air conditioning and electricity switched to reserved power. "Would someone mind explaining to me just *why* the captain had to ask me to let those kids in here?"

"Because-" Konstan grunted, trying to pry the panel off of the control box for the sprinkler system.

"Because what?" Truitt demanded, sending a few engineers to work on the generator.

"Because he needs us to – ouch! – help figure out how to fix Aiyra's brain –"

"What?" Samantha said with a startled laugh.

"Er, I mean, fix the –" He paused for a second, trying to remember what he was talking about. "The implant."

"What implant?"

"A little something the Keltars gave her," Samantha replied, nudging Konstan aside and deftly shutting off the flow of water.

"The Keltars!" Truitt repeated. "Why, my mother was an Irish woman and my father an American, and way back sometime their great-greats had married into the Aithonians, who themselves had been mixed with the remnants of the Keltars. That's how I came to be in engineering," he added. "It was a family trade."

"Uh, yeah, we kind of had figured that part out," Konstan answered distractedly. He was fiddling with a finicky wire that refused to connect its respective circuits. "I mean, not about your parents, about the Keltars and the Aithonians. Any chance you'd know how to disable that implant?"

"Well, I'd have to look at it first. But I'd say there's a good chance of it. I've made a hobby of studying old technology," Truitt admitted, starting to calm down a little as he watched the generator start humming again.

Konstan slammed the panel shut and stood up, wiping his hands on his coat, and then wondered why he bothered. The three of them were soaked; water still dripped from the railings up above them. Clouds of steam left water droplets clinging to their faces and hair.

"They say water and electronics don't mix, but what about engineering?" he grumbled.

"Well, it's practically the same thing in this case. . ." Samantha replied, folding her arms and trying to picture Konstan with a haircut. "Nope."

"What?"

"I was thinking of making you get a haircut." Konstan shook his hair out of his eyes. He grinned at his laughing sister.

"It is getting a bit long," he admitted. "Better get you to trim it! Hey, are *you* growing your hair out on purpose?"

"Huh?"

"I'll take that as a no. It's almost to the middle of your back now," Konstan pointed out. "It looks nice, *sisia*."

"Thanks. Now, we'd better check in on Aiyra!" Samantha exclaimed glancing at her watch. "I hope Elise isn't trying acupuncture on her. Someone tried it on me when I was little – it didn't work for me, and the idea of having needles stuck in you is. . . ouch."

"I'm surprised she thought of that first," Konstan remarked, passing her to get the door. "Hopefully she -" He swung open the door and was knocked flat by an engineering stampede.

"I tried to hold them!" Samantha's acquaintance, Geoffrey, panted. "Did it pretty well for a while! Do you think I might be able to get that job?" Samantha just looked at him for a second.

"Ask Truitt - on second thought, don't ask him. His nerves are fried because his ship is falling apart." Konstan got up from the floor, rubbing his aching neck.

"You can say that again, and mine are near the frying point," he commented. "Come on, Samantha, I need to get to Aiyra."

"Well, I'll walk you to wherever you're going," Geoffrey offered. "If Mr. Yarborough isn't in the mood for interviews, especially with *that* crowd." He glanced over his shoulder at the impatient group awaiting their turn. Truitt had already flung his hands in the air and stormed off.

"No thank you," Konstan declined, beginning to sound as frustrated as he looked.

"I was asking Ms. Anselle," Geoffrey gave him a frigid look.

"I couldn't care less who you were asking!" Konstan growled. Samantha gave him a gentle nudge.

"Go on, Konstan, I'll be right behind you."

Konstan reluctantly set off, with an annoyed glance over his shoulder. He didn't like that Geoffrey was hanging around Samantha; he was likely to annoy her as much as he had just been.

"Look, Geoffrey-" Samantha turned to him, but the boy quickly took her arm and began to walk her down the corridor.

"Come on," he said eagerly. "I'm serious, I want to see the ship anyway. I hear that Captain Hesslin was a military hero in the Battle of Maltara! Any ship *he* commands must be amazing."

"Uh. . . I suppose so," Samantha sighed.

"Oh!" Geoffrey exclaimed in excitement. He dragged her over to a computer. "It's a Class B, model 71A! It's one of the best on the market!" He rattled off a long list of specifications.

"Geoffrey-"

"And over there, I've *always* wanted to see one of those!" Geoffrey pulled her into the VR room and demonstrated how it felt to be standing on the edge of a frozen cliff thousands of feet above an angry volcano.

"Geoffrey-"

"And this!" He went off on another detailed explanation of the method of creating false sunlight and a computer-generated sky for the plaza.

"Geoffrey!"

"Yes?" he asked, breathless but content.

"Geoffrey, I have an appointment. It's been very. . . interesting talking with you, but I must go. Look, if you really want to work in Engineering, go talk to Truitt. If you want to work in IT, *still* go talk to Truitt."

"Oh, okay! I'll see you later, then!" he said brightly, and gave her a quick hug before dashing off.

"Ugh," Samantha groaned, and wondered how she had gotten into such a mess. *Truitt had better not hire him . . .*

XIX

Reliable

"There you are!" Marc exclaimed as he crashed into Samantha when they opened the same door from opposite sides.

"What, you haven't made it to the infirmary yet either?" she panted, breathless from running.

"No, the call was a little long. You?"

"No, this way!" Samantha insisted when Marc tried to continue through the door. "That way will take longer. As I just found out." They began walking.

"Thank you for finding out! Is that what kept you?" Marc asked.

"No, it was a boy who decided he has a crush on me, doesn't hide it as much as I would like, and wants a job as an engineer even though he cut half the wires to the engine and I had to fix it. With Konstan and Truitt's help." Samantha's expression was reminiscent of a thundercloud.

"Samantha, what is it with these men and boys?" Marc groaned, with just a hint of a laugh. He caught her shoulders and made her face him. "I'm sorry, dear. I won't let Truitt hire him."

"I highly doubt he would," she grumbled, "he made such a mess." She leaned her head on Marc's shoulder and he held her.

"I suppose," he said, "that I'm not really all that different from them, except that I wouldn't force you to do anything like Medrhos; I wouldn't humiliate you like Rad did; and I still have no idea what that kid's been up to, but hopefully I wouldn't do whatever he's been doing."

"Why, Marc, you're very different from all of them!" Samantha exclaimed. "I trust you. . . and that's more than I've ever said about anyone. And of course, you couldn't *possibly* annoy me as much as that kid does."

"But don't you trust Konstan and Truitt at least, and your family?" Marc said gently.

"Yes, but I trust Konstan as my friend and brother; Truitt as an uncle and my boss; my family as my family. But you –" She dropped her gaze for a second to search for words.

"And I?" Marc prompted.

"You're just. . . you," she said with a smile. "I trust you as if you were all those things. . . I don't know why." Her watch beeped.

"Oh, oh, we've got to get down to Aiyra!" she jumped. "We've been away for an hour already." They hurried towards the infirmary, dodging nurses and officers.

"Marc, what about Aiyra?" Samantha asked suddenly.

"What about her?" he returned, keeping his eyes on the crowded walkway.

"What will she think? Of-of us?"

Marc just laughed, saying, "Don't you know that she orchestrated the whole thing, Samantha? If she hadn't been pulling strings - admit it, neither of us would be talking to each other."

"Well, I did guess," the engineer admitted, "but it's almost as if she purposely gave herself away. She told me that because she couldn't have her mother, she needed me to be her sister. She might as well have put it more bluntly, it seemed so obvious."

"She probably meant for you to think so," Marc agreed, pulling open the glass door to Elise's office. "She's like that when she's had a secret for what she considers too long." The pair looked through the office, but couldn't find Elise or Aiyra.

"Maybe they finished already," Samantha suggested.

"I don't think so. They would have called one of us. At least we know it can't be worse," Marc said cheerfully, and pulled her along. At last they heard Aiyra's laughter coming from a distant room, and found her sitting on a table, drinking coffee and eating doughnuts. Her arms were wrapped with black pads which encased electronic nerve stimulators; the wires connected it to the computer which kept track of the reactions.

"What's this, second breakfast?" Marc teased, breaking off half the doughnut and splitting it with Samantha.

"At least we know your arms are working since you can eat!" Samantha added, wondering how it was possible to fit whole blackberries inside of a watermelon-flavored doughnut.

"My arms are still rather numb," Aiyra confessed, "but I can move them. I am just glad that the implant is not ruining any computers right now!"

Marc put his arm around her and mischievously dunked his doughnut into her coffee. Laughing, she swatted his hand away.

"Wait –" said Samantha, as Elise finally stepped away from the computer. "Where's Konstan? He left before I did. I thought he would have been here by now; he was so anxious to get back to Aiyra."

"I haven't seen him," Elise replied. "But given the fact that we were on emergency power a few minutes ago, it's highly probable he was stopped for a job."

"How long does Aiyra need to stay?" Marc asked, noticing Aiyra's expression.

"Not long; her nerves should be working well within a few minutes."

"Alright, we'll go find Konstan when you're done," Marc whispered in his daughter's ear. She leaned her head on his shoulder and smiled at Samantha.

~~~

"No, it goes over *there*," Konstan said patiently for the eightieth time. The kitchen workers at Galaxy Café knew nothing about the electronic appliances they used every day, much less where everything went after a fuse had blown and all the outlets had fried.

"Honestly," the engineer muttered, putting his shoulder to the freezer, "how is it that I, who have eaten here only once, know where everything goes and y'all don't?"

"Good memory," one server guessed.

"Nah, good brain food," another insisted, downing the remainder of the blueberry smoothie that sat awaiting for the blender and dispenser to be reset.

"Common sense," Konstan sighed. "I think."

"I'm sure you're thinking properly," Marc said from behind him. He aided Konstan in shoving the freezer back against the wall. One of the waitresses saw the captain and fainted; apparently even a few on his own ship thought of him as a rock star. Even though he hadn't heard one note – if there ever were any notes in the modern version of the genre – of rock in his life. Marc looked over at her.

"What's wrong with her?" he asked dryly.

"Perhaps she is ill," Aiyra suggested with concern. Konstan stopped short and looked at her.

"I doubt it - there you are!" he said with relief. "I was on my way to the infirmary to see you when I got interrupted." He laid aside the tools he had just grabbed to fix a few of the appliances.

"I'm so sorry about that - how are you?" he asked anxiously. Smiling, Aiyra raised both hands and laughingly waved her fingers at him. Konstan laughed and caught her hands.

"You remind me of a space octopus," he teased.

"A space *octopus*? There aren't octopi in space, silly!" Aiyra protested.

"Who says? I've seen 'em once or twice; they like to live in interstellar clouds. I guess it could be compared to the sea for them, but they feed on the energy from the chemical reactions rather than on fish and such," Konstan explained.

"How big are they?"

"Oh, about six inches to a foot, at least the ones I saw," Konstan said cheerfully. "They're rather cute little things; they glow ice-blue with the energy they consume."

"Cute and little!" Marc repeated, coming over. He noticed that Konstan was still holding Aiyra's hands. "Hm. Well, I saw one that was *twelve* feet long, emitting so much residual energy that it half-melted a patch on the *Lumenara's* hull; you can still see it up top."

"Twelve feet! Are you sure you aren't telling fish stories, Captain?" Konstan asked mischievously, pulling on his gloves again as he remembered he had a job to finish.

"Haha, maybe just a slight exaggeration," Marc admitted. "That reminds me – Commander Flynn gave us a new mission to rendezvous on Wednesday with the *Delta IV* in the system of Soltarra. Angel-girl, I think it might be good if you stayed here. . . with your mother."

A look of distress flickered briefly in Aiyra's eyes. "I want to be with you," she said quietly. "A'da, nothing can bring A'ma back to me; but I will not leave you! If I must lose you, I will be there."

Her father looked confused. "I know, sweetheart, but you're not well yet; I'll have Elise stay with you."

"You need a doctor for the refugees," Aiyra reminded him. "She cannot stay with me. Neither can Samantha or Truitt."

Marc exhaled and looked into her eyes, so grave and earnest.

"Will you be okay?" he asked. She nodded. Feeling a sudden sense of relief, Marc said that he would call Commander Flynn and let him know that they could leave sooner than expected. He tried to turn on his com-watch but it short-circuited with a noisy *zap*, leaving the captain's arm tingling for a few moments.

"Well," he gasped, "I guess that proves that water-proofing hasn't been perfected yet. Even in the space generation nothing works!"

"Properly, anyway," Konstan said with a shake of his head, grabbing his bag. He was just glad he didn't have to deal with any more dripping smoothie machines or red-hot toasters. "Here, sir, you can use the ISC."

The engineer pulled out the key for the Interstellar Communications transceiver. Being slightly out of date, they were usually used by personnel who needed to contact home base for advice, whether it was for correcting a recipe, fixing blown fuses, or learning how to play the piano for one of the clubs onboard. Konstan walked over to the wall, only to find that someone had clearly labeled the device "SPACE PHONE." He stared at it.

"Space phone? *Space* phone? Seriously! A *space phone?* Who comes up with this stuff?!"

"Well. . . . it's not as if it's *not* a space phone," Marc laughed. Aiyra came over to look at it.

"They could have called it anything to do with space," she remarked. "Maybe even a galaxy phone since you can use it to call anyone anywhere?"

"Nah, there was a galaxy phone ages ago; and then there was that black-hole phone that sucked everyone's time away because they were always staring at it, and supposedly that made it smart," Konstan replied, unscrewing the plates, and fiddled with the wiring.

"I've got a better idea," Marc said dryly. "Why don't we just call it a phone since a phone is a phone by any name?"

"Fan-*tastic* idea!" Konstan grunted. "And after that, let's change the names of all those strange foods being served in the cafeteria so that they actually sound edible."

"Oh, like the space pasta?" Aiyra inquired.

"Yeah, and what about this one: 'Wormhole Churros filled with Comet Custard.'"

"Let's not forget the infamous 'Oort Cloud Meringue with Anti-Matter Pudding and Red Giant Cherries,'" Marc added. "Can't we get any normal-sounding things around here?"

"That reminds me," Aiyra said suddenly. "I heard somebody talking about cherry-cheese pizza." The other two stopped and stared at her.

"OK, that's even weirder right there," said Konstan, waving his screwdriver. "Uh, I'll take the 'Wormhole Churros,' please, just so long as they don't serve me *that.*"

Aiyra blinked. "I thought it sounded kind of interesting."

Konstan stopped and looked at her again. "OK, tell you what – if you eat the 'Wormhole Churros,' I'll eat the cherry-cheese pizza."

"But I wanted to eat the pizza, and you just said *you* wanted to eat the churros!" she objected. Marc just laughed at them both and put in the call once Konstan had replaced the cover. It took a few minutes for the call to reach across the quadrant to headquarters. Commander Flynn was happy to hear that Aiyra was better.

"Still, no rush, Captain. I just received word that the *Delta IV* is investigating a call that came through a few hours ago; it'll be another day before they reach the rendezvous point," Flynn told him. "And incidentally, why are you using the ISC? It's been ages since I got a call on one of those."

"Uh. . . I accidentally, or maybe not so accidentally, took a swim in the ocean last night. My com-watch was supposedly waterproof, but it finally went out on me a few minutes ago, and I didn't want to take the time to walk to my cabin," Marc said sheepishly.

"Hm, it sounds like you aren't doing half as bad as I thought you would be," Flynn laughed. "You wouldn't be going for a swim if you were *that* miserable. A man wouldn't be able to consider enjoying himself. No, I have a suspicious feeling that there's someone around to cheer you up after all that you've been through. Don't lose her, Marc; whoever she is, she's good for you. Talk to you later." He signed off before Marc had a chance to reply.

"Eh. . . guess I'd better not," he muttered to himself, but he was smiling. "Now, you two, what about that cherry-cheese pizza and those churros?"

XX

Breakthrough

Samantha warily entered the IT break room. Truitt was occupying a window seat and sipping his coffee as he read the latest tech reports from the Vestar Fleet. A few technicians, engineers, and security officers were chatting in the corner, but it was relatively quiet for the lunch hour; likely due to the *Lumenara's* imminent departure from Maedra. Samantha slipped into a seat next to Truitt.

"What gives?" she asked in a low voice.

"About what?" asked Truitt, leisurely flipping the page. *Man, do I need a break,* he thought.

"About the new recruits. I hope . . . there were a few good prospects? Since we're leaving, I mean," she explained.

"Yes, I know exactly what you mean. There were a couple decent kids there, and a few old hands," Truitt replied, flinging the magazine aside and wondering who in their right mind would have written that every man in space should wear a virtual headset. *Talk about a lack of concentration!*

"You didn't hire Geoffrey, I hope?" Samantha asked anxiously.

"Certainly not!" Truitt dropped his now empty hands on the table and rocked his coffee cup. He hastily steadied it. "How could I, after I saw Konstan get furious with him? When he gets angry at someone, you can bet there is *no* good reason for having that particular someone hang around."

"Wait, Konstan was arguing with him?" Samantha repeated. "What was he angry about?"

"Geoffrey's behavior – what else?" Truitt shrugged. "He told me he was sick of Geoffrey claiming that you were his girlfriend. Are you surprised?"

"In that case, no," Samantha muttered, running her fingers through her hair. "Speaking of Konstan, where is he? Working on Sergeant Raye's filing system again?"

"No, he ran past me a few minutes ago saying he had an idea about something. He finished the filing this morning; I believe he's in the lab."

Samantha thanked him and head out. She poked her head into the lab and found Konstan putting together a few pieces of circuitry which she recognized from Marc's former computer.

"Hey," she said. "Thanks for sending Geoffrey away."

"No problem," Konstan snorted, without looking up. "It was my pleasure!"

Samantha peered over his shoulder. "What are you working on?"

Konstan's eyes smiled and he flipped a switch.

~~~

Aiyra watched as Maedra spun away below her. She was standing in the lower observation deck which hung from the belly of the ship. A swirl of ocean and sand with a splash of white – she felt mixed emotions as she lost sight of the dark cliffs and the church where her mother's body had lain for centuries. Or was it five years? She shuddered a moment and cringed as a faint shock ran through the nerves in her head.

It was early Tuesday morning, Maedrean time, but Monday morning in SVT, or Standardized Vestar Time, which was based on Earth time. They were on their way to their Wednesday rendezvous – SVT. The door slid open behind her.

"Darling, I do wish you'd lie down!" her father said, entering. "You're not quite well yet. The idea of you getting sick because you're standing on a glass floor over a spinning planet scares me." He put his arm around her and drew her aside.

"I have some good news," he offered. "Samantha, Truitt, and Konstan think they've figured out a way to permanently disable and eventually remove the implant. It'll take a few days for Elise to make ready for the procedure, however. It should work." Aiyra said nothing, but turned her head towards him. It was so hard to struggle out of her own thoughts sometimes.

"Thank you, A'da. I hope it will!" she sighed. "Ever since Konstan was able to turn it off, I feel as though I have lost half the energy of my brain."

"I don't know why that would be," Marc said uncertainly. "I would have thought it would be the opposite. Come on, maybe you need to rest." He took her hand and led her off the deck.

~~~

Beep. Beep. Beep.

"Let's hope it works!" Samantha said, straightening and setting the device in the chamber. She shoved the door shut and Konstan locked it. The pair had spent nearly twenty hours on the project now. Would it work?

"How will we know if it does?" Samantha asked him.

"If it returns, I suppose," he replied, his eyes on the device as he handled the remote. He pressed the *send* button. The lights flashed, the air inside the chamber wavered, and it was gone. There were several minutes of silence.

"It should be back a few minutes ago," Konstan muttered, his eyes locked on the chamber.

"Then it should be returning any second now!" Samantha watched anxiously. The pair had put many long hours into this device and such tests – would this one be fruitless as well? Then a sudden flash of smoldering light, and the device was again in the chamber, its lights flashing furiously.

"It worked!" Konstan cried jubilantly. "Call the captain; he ought to come down here."

~~~

"So, what is this about?" Marc asked, eyeing the tiny devices which were reminiscent of a satellite that had collided with an old smartphone.

"In theory, these are transceivers which can be used to locate someone, were they to be caught in a time rift," Konstan replied. "Basically, the time rifts are just a different dimension, not a different location; so the trackers will hopefully be able to pinpoint both time and location, so that we could navigate the fields of Borania if necessary."

"That's a lot of ifs!" Marc commented. "But I still don't quite get how you managed to come up with something that *might* work."

"Well, we figured that we can't use satellites," Samantha explained. "We can't count on them existing in the past *or* the future. And we aren't in orbit, anyway. These radio transceivers utilize any light found in space – stars, solar flares, ultraviolet light. In order for this to work properly for our purposes, the coordinates would have to be triangulated. So, for now, I have one, Konstan has one, and here – now you have one. If you were searching for me, you could narrow the range until you get a close approximation of where I am, as long as I have the tracker with me. This is just a small scale, though; ideally, there would be one on the *Lumenara*."

"If this works," Konstan interjected, "the *Lumenara's* radio can probably be tuned to receive the same frequency as these transceivers use. Samantha and I want to modify it to incorporate a scanner that will allow them to digitally tune through all frequencies in use. That way, if one of the trackers was accidentally reset, it could still be located."

"Wait, tell me again: how did you manage to test them and know that it will work to track something in a different time period?"

"We could have sent it out to Borania, but figuring that no one would appreciate that, we probably chose the more dangerous route," Samantha said, staring into the chamber and bracing herself.

"We reconstructed the conditions of the time warp fields in the chamber," Konstan stated.

"You did *what* in my ship?!" Marc spluttered. "Do you have any idea what could happen if that chamber malfunctioned and those 'conditions' spread throughout the *Lumenara*? And incidentally, how does it work?" The sudden transition between anger and innocent curiosity made both engineers choke on a laugh.

"The Vestar Fleet sent us some scans and test results taken in the fields," Konstan said, managing a straight face. "We copied the conditions into the chamber, including the energy levels, gases, and molecular activity of the clouds found in Borania. It's near enough to the real thing for us to say that these trackers have an 95% guarantee to function properly *if* they were to be used in the way intended." Marc stared into the swirling electric blue and cherry-rose cloud contained in the chamber.

"Why didn't you tell me you were doing this?"

"Because I didn't want you to think you could test it out on yourself." Samantha's eyes were locked on him, like a cat that knows exactly what a human is thinking.

Marc stared back. They hadn't tested it on anything but the trackers themselves – how could they know whether it would work on humans? His mind began to race.

"Don't even think about it." Samantha's hand slid to a small stun gun in a holster at her side. She had never worn it before. It was evident that she knew just how hard Marc would have to fight the temptation to leap into the chamber.

"Samantha. You need to test it on a human subject in order to know that it will work."

"Captain. You were furious a few seconds ago that we even had done this on your ship. Now you are prepared to let your daughter, your crew, your friends, and the Vestar Fleet to potentially lose you for good?"

"Samantha, as your captain I think I can choose to be a test subject if I wish," Marc said coolly, his heart beating fast. "It's your experiment. If I blow up or choke to death, or get lost in time. . . ." He wasn't angry with her, nor even doubting the fact that the controlled test was perfectly safe; but his whole mind was bent upon finding a way into that chamber and back to Talitha.

"If you enter that chamber, Marc, and go back to your old life, you will no longer be my captain - and I won't have to listen to you," Samantha replied.

Konstan was staring at them both. "Maybe this wasn't such a good idea after all," he muttered, his eyes hastily scanning the controls. He discreetly disabled the computer and it began to delete all memory of the chamber's current conditions. But Marc reached for the door.

"Don't you dare!" said Samantha. Suddenly the pistol was directed towards him and the three went very still. "Don't test me, Marc." A few tense seconds ticked by. Marc didn't seem to notice the gas rapidly vanishing from inside the chamber. Konstan breathed a sigh of relief. The door slid open.

"What in thunder-" gasped Truitt, seeing Marc and Samantha glaring at each other at opposite ends of a gun. "Samantha!" He pulled the pistol from her hand, gently slapping her wrist as he did so. "What's wrong with you? Last I saw you, you were holding hands; now you're ready to stun him? Come on, both of you, you could use some time out!"

He took their arms and took them out into the hall. He proceeded to place Samantha's hand in Marc's and sent them down the corridor without bothering to ask for an explanation. He knew he could get it from Konstan with less confusion and fewer excuses. Marc and Samantha looked uncertainly over their shoulders like two schoolchildren sentenced to stand in a corner all day. Truitt shooed them off. Marc pulled his companion along. Silence.

"Marc-"

"It's fine. I'm sorry for acting that way; I knew better than to try and get into that chamber. Talitha told me not to look for her," Marc sighed. He squeezed her hand. "And I told you that I was no longer tempted. . . because I know now that you need me. I can only imagine how I just made you feel, Samantha. Will you forgive me?"

"It's alright, Marc, I didn't feel it. I was too busy feeling *your* pain. I'm sorry, and not sorry, that I was going to stun you," Samantha murmured. "I just didn't want to lose you, Marc." He just laughed.

"Now I know you really love me," he joked. "Enough to stun me rather than let me potentially blow myself up with your own experiment. Tell Konstan to delete the conditions for the fields. . . I know I'll try it again, even if it's in my sleep."

"He already did," Samantha smiled. "While you were busy staring at my pistol, silly. Did you really think I was angry and about to fire at you? Konstan and I had planned for emergencies." She bumped him playfully, and he pushed her back.

"You noodle! Did you really think that *I* would think that you would fire at me? I saw Konstan fiddling with the controls. Come on, let's get back to work. I need to check on Aiyra; for now, we'll forget about experimenting with the trackers. If someone gets lost, hopefully we'll find that the transceivers work the way you planned."

Hopefully we won't have to find out, Samantha thought.

XXI

Destruction

The *Lumenara* glided swiftly towards Soltarra, navigating the system's extensive asteroid belt. There were seven planets of varying hues and environments – Erimos, Xiroz, Ammost, Zesto, Atmos, Lythos, and Elinikos - but none of them habitable. This rendered it as a generally accepted neutral zone, with a few sparsely populated research facilities and satellite outposts. This was the only reason that they could meet with the *Delta IV* here; the ship was so heavily weighted and its mission so long, that they were running low on energy with most of it being rerouted to the infirmary, kitchens, and life support. They could only manage 300 c, which was only half of the recommended cruising speed for interstellar travel.

Being in unfamiliar territory, Marc spent much of his time on the bridge. Aiyra, meanwhile, spent most of her time in the infirmary. Elise was preparing for the procedure which Konstan and Samantha believed might enable them to permanently disable and remove the implant. Marc had to resist the urge to call down to them every few minutes to make sure that all was well; of course it was. Instead, he busied himself with putting a call through to Lord Ransomme. There were a few intermittent beeps. Then nothing.

"Vidara, did the call reach them?" Marc asked, studying the seven planets that lay before them. His communications officer couldn't tell.

"From the looks of it, I would guess that they aren't in range, sir," she replied.

"How can that be? They should have been here several hours ago!" the captain muttered. "There's probably some interference from the satellites, then. Briggs, run a scan of Soltarra and tell me if the *Delta* is anywhere in it." Briggs tapped away and the lights on the *Lumenara's* hull flashed.

"The *Delta* does not appear to be – wait. There is a ship sitting behind the far moon of Lythos," he noted. "It's too far away for me to tell whether it's the *Delta*."

"Lythos is nearest the sun," Vidara commented. "That, and being behind the planet, could explain why the call didn't go through."

"*If* it's the *Delta*," Marc said. "It could be a research vessel; there shouldn't be any other ships in the area. Let's get closer."

Marc felt his heart beating faster as they approached Lythos, and wasn't sure why; he grew tense and silence fell on the bridge. Now they were coming around the dark side of the desert planet, with its shrouded plateaus and river-run canyons. Darkness fell over them, and the lights in the ship flickered briefly. There, with the sun glinting off her hull, yet nearly hidden in the shadow of Lythos, There was a sudden anxious beeping, a very familiar signal – a distress call, coming from the ship!

"Call them," Marc ordered Vidara. "Ask them what's wrong and what they need." Vidara put the call through, but there was a strange silence and no answer.

"What ship is it?" Marc asked tersely.

"The *U.S.C. Remnant*, sir," Vidara replied. "A relatively ancient 'A' class ship from approximately three hundred years ago. The fleet's records state that it was an old colonizing ship which vanished after a century of failed colonization attempts."

"Any life signs?"

"No sir," Briggs said quietly. "But our sensors are now picking up a second ship docked with the *Remnant*. It's the *Delta*." Marc stared at the ship before him; the *Lumenara's* cruising speed quickly brought the *Delta IV* into sight. Marc was almost afraid to ask.

"Life signs?"

"None."

Marc felt a chill creeping up his spine. Where could everyone have gone? Where could 200 knights, officers, and workers and 3,000 refugees hide? Lythos was a possibility, but neither of the dead ships held enough escape pods to carry all the passengers.

"Wait a minute," Briggs said slowly, staring at the touchscreen before him. "Sir, there's another ship behind the *Remnant*, and it's coming up fast-"

No sooner had he gotten these words out when a flash of silver and scarlet shot for them like sprite lightning from a thundercloud. It was a X-19 Starkindler, a heavy spacefighter almost half the size of the *Lumenara*. It bore the crest of the Marauders – a crescent moon hung with fire and waves, and a bleeding sword that gleamed red.

"Get the shields up!" Briggs cried, panicking.

"We don't have any! The fleet still hasn't found a working one," Pell snapped.

"Get us out of here!" Marc ordered. If the fighter fired, though it couldn't take every passenger captive, the *Lumenara* would be crippled just as the *Delta* and *Remnant* appeared to have been. A blast of laser fire rocked the ship as the Starkindler skimmed overhead. Ensign Topping quickly brought the ship about and aimed for the asteroid belt for a hasty retreat, taking the speed up to 900 *c*. But the Starkindler possessed greater speed, and its agility made it capable of taking out two of the six nacelles located on the underside of the hull. These nacelles alternated between fuel containers, engines, and energy cells for powering them.

"Sir, we're losing fuel from nacelle 3, and nacelle 6 is out! One of the engines is down," Briggs informed him. The *Lumenara* continued to coast at 800 *c*, and would do so for several minutes; but they were losing their ability to even make 500 *c*.

"If we don't get out of here that fighter will call in reinforcements," Pell warned.

"Then fire back!" Marc replied. He punched the 'call' button on the computer panel before him.

"Hesslin to Engineering! Truitt, what's up?" There was a crackle and a brief delay.

"We're working on the engine, Captain, but you'll have to either get us out of here or destroy that fighter! The programming lock on nacelle 6 is malfunctioning, so I'm going to need to send Konstan to work on it from the outside."

"I can give you five minutes," Marc replied. He was watching the Starkindler dance in and out of range of the *Lumenara's* HF lasers.

"Try the tractor beam!" Pell said. "We might be able to paralyze it." Again, the Starkindler was too swift. Explosions were occurring all over the *Lumenara's* hull.

"Go, Konstan!" Marc muttered, trying to keep his crew together. "You're the only one who can get us out of here now!"

~~~

"And after you get past the code, remove the grid on the far side of the engine, replace the isolator and energy cell, and –"

"Yeah, yeah, I know, avoid getting blown up!" Konstan panted. He and Truitt were running down the hall, taking the stairs between the floors two at a time. The lights flashed overhead, for the generators were being knocked out, one by one, though the Starkindler had endured several near-direct hits.

"Konstan!" The desperate voice dragged the engineer to a halt. Aiyra stood panting in the doorway of the infirmary, having thrown herself from the examination table when she heard what was happening. Konstan seized her hands and looked lovingly into her eyes, so concerned and gentle.

"Konstan! If you go, I will lose you," she whispered.

"If I don't, we'll all lose each other," he replied.

"I know. You are a third of my world and my Daystar, Konstan." Konstan smiled and touched her dark hair.

"And you're a third of mine, my Aurora! We'll be fine, Princess. Like we always have to be, remember? I'll come back to you, even if I'm not in one piece, even if it takes a thousand years. And I'll help you. . . I promise."

"I remember. God-speed and may He be your shield!" Aiyra replied, and pressed something into his hand. Konstan threw his arms around her and held her tight for a moment before Truitt dragged him down the corridor.

~~~

"Truitt, your five minutes are almost up!" Marc shouted into the receiver as he heard another explosion somewhere above him. The *Lumenara* would either shatter like a glass or explode like a gas giant if they didn't take down the Starkindler first.

"I know! Konstan's almost through!" Truitt barked, his nerves straining as he tried to keep the ship together.

Konstan heard the exchange over his headset. Clothed in a close-fitting pressurized suit, he was struggling to get the engine of nacelle 6 back into the game. He had managed to loosen the grid and replace the isolator, but the energy cell was a different matter entirely. To speed things up, he had already turned it on. It glowed a violent blue, and nearly burned his hands through his gloves, making it difficult to both hold and lock in place. There were seven locks to pin it down, but it took one hand to keep the cell from floating away and nearly required two to turn each lock. But finally! The last snapped in place!

"I got it! Get it running, Truitt!" he cried, and shoving the door shut, began the slow climb up the hull to the service airlock. He looked up and vaguely saw a figure in white and another in green, and knew that Aiyra and Samantha were watching him, nerves straining as though they were making the climb themselves. He raised his hand and waved to them as he reached for the last rung –

A burst of icy flame, orange lasers, and golden sparks, and the side of the *Lumenara* imploded. Aiyra and Samantha were thrown back into the wall, and Samantha slid from the platform and fell to the floor twenty feet below. Her companion was caught in the net of live wires from an exploded electrical panel. Aiyra screamed but not because of the pain. Konstan was gone.

XXII

Lost

Samantha shoved herself into a sitting position. Her body ached all over and her head swam. Everywhere she saw flames, smoke, steam, sparks. A worker ran towards her and helped her stand.

"I'll get you to the infirmary," he offered. Samantha shook her head with a breathless thank-you. There was no time for her injuries now, not when she was needed, not when Aiyra was hurt.

"Aiyra. . . Aiyra," she muttered, and dragged herself up the stairs. Somehow Aiyra had disentangled herself and was trying to navigate the wreckage-strewn pathway. Samantha grabbed her and helped her climb over a fallen beam. The girl's sense of direction and balance were completely twisted and she seemed to be fading in and out of consciousness while remaining on her feet. Another shot from the Starkindler nearly threw them to the ground again.

"There's a second fighter out there," Samantha said grimly. "We need to get out of here!" Supporting each other, the pair made it to the nearest intercom.

"Samantha to Hesslin," she panted. "Marc, there's a second ship. We lost Konstan." There was a momentary silence and Samantha almost wondered whether the system was working.

"I have one last idea of how to get out of here," Marc's voice came back. "Samantha, get Truitt to empty the cargo bay."

~~~

The Starkindlers teamed up. The *Lumenara* was limping now; it was so heavily damaged that it could hardly have a chance for escape. She was an easy prey. The fighters split off from each other and came around in a wide arc towards the port and starboard sides of the ship. One last barrage would do it. They took aim and drew their lasers across the underside of the ship, striking the other four nacelles and the cargo bay doors.

There was a flash of fire and a wave of energy that caused both fighter ships to shake. The carcass of the *Lumenara* began to roll slowly, drawn in by Lythos like a ship in a maelstrom. The artificial gravity was lost – and the hull, torn open, bled trash and laundry, carpets and tiling, lamps and bedding, garden plants and kitchen scraps, waste and chemical gases. A faint cloud of nitrogen poured from the aft of the *Lumenara*, a leak sprung in her tanks of fuel. Marc's plan had come too late; the ship had lost the battle forever.

The Starkindlers pulled off, navigating the flotsam, and watched as the wreckage began to accelerate towards the atmosphere of the planet. It was a job well-done, though it would have been better done with survivors. No matter. . . . Medrhos wanted no one to interfere, and if that's what he wanted, that's what he would get. The fighters abandoned the scene, with no evidence left behind but the wreckage far below, ready to settle in the dust of Lythos. . . just another tale lost in time.

XXIII

Broken

The desert sun beat down upon the smoldering carcass of the once-beautiful *Lumenara*. A dead breeze scarcely grazed the dunes that fell from the cliffs and plateaus, as though the bare rock were a monolithic beast perpetually rising from slumbering sand. Desert boas and sand rats slithered and scurried in the shadows of the sunken landscape, looking for an easy meal among the scattered wreckage. They needn't have bothered. The only free meal they would be getting were any table scraps that chanced to have escaped the cargo bay after the ship had entered the thin atmosphere.

Marc drew himself to his feet, his back aching and his bones feeling as though they had been tossed through a rock tumbler for an hour before being reassembled. He looked around. Most of his crew were sitting dazedly at their posts, though a few were still shaking themselves awake.

A shower of sparks was falling from a smashed interface and the emergency sprinklers had switched on. The plumbing must have been damaged, though, as the flow of water was thinning until it was only a trickle. Thankfully, this time they weren't directed at the computers. He was relieved to see that this seemed to be the extent of the damage to the bridge. If he hadn't recalled an old Earth story of an ocean vessel, the *Lumenara* likely would have blown up. But the trick of using garbage and flotsam to create the look of an explosion, and turning off the artificial gravity and all the ship's power had saved them.

"Pell?" Marc asked tersely. The First Officer was listening to his headset. He turned to the captain.

"I'm getting reports of numerous minor injuries, Captain, and a few serious ones. There have been two dozen fatalities."

A soft groan escaped Marc's lips and he muttered a prayer for them all. He could only be grateful that the numbers had been no greater.

"And Aiyra?" He waited anxiously as Pell made the inquiry. The officer turned back to him.

"Her injuries are relatively minor. She's trying to help Elise put the infirmary back to rights so that serious injuries can be taken care of."

Marc exhaled in relief and tried to pull himself together. He'd have to go and check on his daughter as soon as he could – but as a captain, first he'd need to make the first few steps of setting things to rights. He added a thanksgiving for the safety of the rest of the crew, and called down to Engineering.

"Hesslin here - Truitt! How bad is it?" He heard coughing on the other end for a minute.

"Pretty bad," Truitt panted. "Your ship's still almost in one piece, though, sir!"

"The idea of adding the unused gases from the engines to the loaded cargo bay is what did it," Marc commended him.

"That was all Samantha," Truitt replied. "That added to the load of laundry and trash makes a trick the fleet will want to remember!"

Samantha's voice came over in the background, mingled with the noise of struggling machinery. "I'm afraid it did damage the hull some; we're pretty scarred by those laser blasts. And the near-crash-landing did a number on every inch of her, too," she informed him. "We won't be going anywhere for a while. However, the damage is mainly superficial. We were able to rig a shield of sorts for the nacelles, so they're mostly undamaged. It's just the hull and a few systems, not to mention the internal state of affairs with the loss of gravity."

"I can imagine," Marc sighed. "What systems are out? We're going to need everyone on this ship to become an engineer in order to get off this planet."

"Air conditioning, plumbing, and half the power. Even with everyone on board working, it'll take us several weeks to get the *Lumenara* off the ground," Samantha answered.

"Alright, let's concentrate on getting all the injured to the infirmary and burying the dead before we start recruiting each other," Marc instructed them. "I'll see you two soon."

He got up and took Vidara's arm. There was a bloody laceration running from her temple to her jawbone, courtesy of the cracked glass of the computer when the rough landing had thrown her against it.

"It looks as bad as though I had drawn it with lipstick," Vidara smiled weakly, glancing at her shadowy reflection in the broken screen.

"Come on, I'll get you down to the infirmary," Marc said kindly. Ever since Pell and his niece had become part of his crew, Vidara had been like a daughter to him, and he always looked out for her. This was no exception.

Supporting her, he led her and Ensign Topping, who had received several serious bruises when the impact had slammed him against the interface, out of the bridge and down to the plaza. They saw a deluge of sparks in more than one corner, singed and drooping plants in the garden, burst water pipes, and most of all, a topsy-turvy world with chairs on counters, paintings on the floor, and carpets cast over beams as though they had been caught in the act of flying.

Marc shook his head at the damage. At least if they could get a crew together to set furnishings back in place, the work would look like less. The state of the infirmary just added to Marc's stress: most of the power was out; several of the instruments had been smashed; half the medical supplies had been either burned, soaked by the sprinklers, or crushed; and examination tables had been flipped upside-down.

Elise had her hands full with burns, bruises, broken bones, and lacerations, yet somehow she managed to remain calm. Aiyra alternately aided in straightening up the rooms and in filling in for Elise wherever she could; it didn't take a rocket scientist to see that the girl was falling back into her old ways of distracting herself from her own pain. Konstan's death was like a star that had suddenly gone out when its light was all there was. A nurse came and took Vidara and Topping to a separate room where they could be treated. Aiyra looked up to see what was next on her plate and saw her father.

"Aiyra!" Marc called softly, and scrambled over a fallen shelving unit to get to her. He held his daughter tight. He could feel her heart racing as his embrace threatened to draw out the tears she was holding back. Aiyra pressed her head against his shoulder.

"Konstan was a lot to all of us," Marc whispered to her. "He was everyone's brother. . . and almost like a son. You know he still loves you, Aiyra."

The girl nodded and straightened, pulling her hair back. Marc gently inspected the electrical burns on his daughter's neck and hands. Thankfully the Cythian fabric in her robe was woven with quartz crystals, which had helped protect her from some of the electrical shock she had received. She was just a bit weak and still in a slight daze. Elise had already treated her as best as she could with the depleted supplies; now the girl needed some rest. She wouldn't want to take any, but he knew he could convince her in a roundabout way.

"When you're done helping Elise, I want you to go check on the chapel and see what damage there is," Marc told her. This brought a flicker of a smile to his daughter's face.

"Thank you, A'da," she said, and returned to her work.

~~~

An hour later found Aiyra picking her way through the debris on Level 10. The place she loved so well, with its meditation gardens, libraries, plaza, and the beautiful chapel, large enough to hold more than half of the crew at once, was buried. Dust, torn garden plants, mud from the broken hydroponics system, and smashed statues scattered the floor.

Aiyra came to the chapel door and found something was leaning against the doors inside. She put her shoulder to it and managed to shove it open far enough to slip in. It was the massive holy water font with its carved angels that lay on its side, the blessed water having spilled and seeped into the embroidered carpet in the entryway.

A few statues had fallen; potted plants were scattered everywhere, upside-down as though trying to create artistic patterns of dirt on the tiled floors. A pillar had snapped in the crash, and in falling, smashed the communion rail and narrowly missed the altar. A few of the stained-glass faux windows had shattered. Yet, the tabernacle had remained entirely unscathed. The monstrance had somehow remained in place despite the loss of gravity.

Aiyra breathed a sigh of relief and found a little light stealing through the clouds in her heart. The feeling she had had upon first entering this blessed place only a month before returned. Here was her home, for here was the only One who had left His home to be with her. And where He was, so was Konstan.

XXIV

Stranded

The sun beat down on the hull of the *Lumenara*, blinding those who took refuge from the heat in the crevasses of the cliffs, and roasting those unfortunate enough to be inside the ship. It had been three weeks since the battle, and the air conditioning still wasn't fixed. The spare parts had either been lost, misplaced amongst the flotsam jettisoned in space, or melted down in the recycling facility. They would have to be manufactured. The once energetic and well-dressed crew, now scarcely able to walk without staggering in the heat, had been forced to shed a layer or two. They looked like something out of one of those ancient 'lost in the desert' movies, but now they knew what it was like.

Nerves were fraying, patience stretched, and tempers scarcely checked. Yet the crew somehow managed to remember that they had more reason to survive than to just escape the heat, and held themselves together better than could be expected. Those who couldn't bear the heat inside set up camp, as said, in the shadows of the overhanging cliffs, small caves, and monumental fissures. The ship had been cleaned out and most of the interior set to rights, at least where cleaning and organization was concerned; but the hull was still in need of extensive patchwork.

Marc had put himself to work. Not only did he do his best to keep everyone as cheerful and organized as possible, but he helped with anything and everything. Today he was helping with work on the

187

Lumenara's hull. The explosions, crash-landing, and dust storms had scarred the silver plating. Though still bright enough to hurt one's eyes, it was no longer reflective enough to help cool the inside of the ship.

Sweat poured down Marc's face and arms in torrents, drenching his hair and white shirt. The metal burned his hands even through the protective gloves he wore. Crouched on the side of the ship, he slammed metal sheets into place, riveted them, and torched the edges until it molded to the curvature of the hull. Something in the welding gun fried; and then Marc ran out of rivets. He still didn't have a new com-watch, so he had to pass the message on down the outer levels of the ship. He spent nearly an hour trying not to die of heat stroke while he waited. He finally gave up.

Getting to his feet, he used the quickest route down from the 21st level. He jumped. Sliding down the side of the towering ship would have been fun at any other time, but it felt like he was on a lava slide, and had to adjust his trajectory every split-second to avoid crashing through a weak spot in the plating. He landed on the sand and nearly crashed into Samantha.

Her ivory blouse and olive skirt were stained, yet her hair somehow managed to be perfect, as usual, without her trying. But her expression was such that she seemed to have had all her energy and emotion removed from her. That, combined with the exhaustion and the heat, made her look sullen. She held out the rivets and the pieces for the welding gun.

"I suppose you won't want to be using them now," she stated. "You've been out a little long, Captain." Marc took the supplies from her and sent them to another worker.

"Come on," he said wearily. "You're right, I need to get inside. Though that's not much better." Together they crossed the sand and entered the passenger gate. Samantha stumbled a bit, and Marc pulled her back upright.

"Samantha-" he looked at her face and realized why she looked so out of it. She wasn't even sweating. Her breathing was coming strangely, and when he held her wrist, he could feel her pulse was up. She was having the heat stroke that he had somehow managed to avoid.

"Come with me," he murmured, taking her hand. "You're in no condition to be working!" He borrowed an onboard scooter, generally used by maintenance, and drove Samantha down to the infirmary. Elise, luckily, had been able to get most of her patients back on their feet and was enjoying a little quiet time. She took one look at Samantha and ordered her into one of the beds.

"But I can work," the engineer protested. She was stubborn.

"You lie still, or else!" Elise said sternly. She dampened a sheet and spread it over the engineer, placing ice around her body. "I happen to know that you've worked three weeks straight with too little rest; you're so dehydrated I'm amazed you lasted this long."

"Almedrans don't take the heat very well," Samantha mumbled sheepishly.

But from the time he had seen her just a few minutes ago, she seemed to have lost what little energy she had left. Marc stood by anxiously as he watched Elise try to give Samantha a re-hydration drink. The engineer was too tired.

"Captain, you really need to get the air conditioning fixed," the doctor sighed, coming away from the bedside.

"I know," Marc muttered. "I'll call down to the lab and see if they were able to accomplish anything."

Upon finding that they were short-handed, the captain pulled most of the crew in and sent half of them to work on the hydraulics system and the plumbing, which would help cool things down a bit. The rest put themselves to work helping to create and test the necessary parts for the ship. Marc hesitated to leave. Samantha was so pale that he worried.

"You can stay," Elise said, upon seeing his anxiety. "You were out in the heat a little long yourself. I'd like to keep an eye on you." She tossed him the drink that Samantha hadn't even tasted. "Have this, and get a little rest. I'll be back to check on her."

She left to visit her other patients. Marc took a sip of the drink. It tasted like weak lemonade, but with salt and electrolytes added. He leaned his head back against the wall.

Would they get off this planet? That depended on the *Lumenara* – would she get off the ground, or would they have to attempt to carve a habitable oasis out from under her hull? More importantly, would the crew survive? And would Samantha be alright?

He had noticed that in those three weeks, as Elise had said, Samantha had buried herself in work again, with hardly a word to him. When she had spoken, she had addressed him only as her captain. All these things, he thought, were probably her reaction to Konstan's death. He sighed and shut his eyes.

He knew how much it hurt both Samantha and Aiyra. The other two dozen dead crew members had received a funeral and temporary burial in the chapel crypt. Konstan, however, would never have a final resting place. Even Talitha had her place. . . deep in the cold, stone church, with its peaceful, flickering candles, softly echoing halls, golden bells, and birds. . . .

He must have fallen asleep then, for the next thing he knew, he was on a carved bench in the church crypt, leaning against a pillar. But no, he was on the *Lumenara*, not on Maedra; the cold he was feeling was the air conditioner! That soft hissing sound was one of the most beautiful things he had ever heard. He jumped up. Samantha stirred, instantly revived by the cold air. A positive side to the Almedran reaction to heatstroke, Marc supposed.

"Let me work!" Samantha said happily, seeing Elise. "I've got to fix up this ship, so I'm going to."

Elise just laughed and shook her head. Samantha managed to get her way eventually, and was soon found contentedly working on the hydraulics system as the overheated crew ran back into the ship for a well-earned rest. Marc left then and helped some of the parents fix up the children's playroom on Level 13; now that the ship had air conditioning, the children would be happy to get some playtime in again.

That afternoon, the crew took a much-needed break. The air conditioning system was working, the chapel had been mostly cleaned up except for repairs, the hull was half-patched, and some progress was being made on the plumbing.

Marc, Samantha, Aiyra, and Truitt were all seated around a table, watching as the rest of the crew began to relax for the first time in weeks. Things would have been made easier if the showers had been usable for cooling off and washing the sand out of one's hair.

"At least some people are happy," Samantha sighed, resting her head on her hand and staring glumly across the room. There was a hole in her heart. Every time she turned her head, she expected to find Konstan at her side, as always, but he wasn't there.

"Thankfully, our losses were few," Truitt said gently. "Thanks to you and the Captain, most of us came through with less than you, Samantha." He squeezed her shoulder.

Marc leaned on the table, hardly able to keep his eyes open, yet so tired that he couldn't help but stay awake. He had hardly gotten in twenty-four hours of sleep in the past two weeks, between working on the ship, keeping the crew together, overseeing every problem that had occurred, and trying to get a message through to Commander Flynn.

The latter had been a complete failure. Even though the communications systems had been fixed, something about Lythos' atmosphere, or what little there was of it, prevented the signal from getting through.

"Has it occurred to anyone," Aiyra said abruptly, "that Konstan has been gone for three weeks? Is he going to have a funeral Mass, or not?"

Marc shook himself and looked at her. Clearly Aiyra still had that nagging feeling about Konstan – that she could hear his voice at night, calling to her as though she could have saved him. Marc sighed and rubbed his forehead. Out of all the dead, Konstan alone had not had his funeral yet, being the only one whose body was not present.

"Yes," he said wearily. "We can have a memorial Mass for him. . . . just as soon as we can get the ship running again." The funny thing was, he couldn't think of a reason for waiting. "Of all the times to not have coffee," he sighed.

"A'da," Aiyra whispered, reaching out. "Sooner is better, and it will not stop anyone from working."

"Not now," Marc muttered, leaning his head on her shoulder.

"No, not now," Aiyra repeated. "Just soon. Are you alright, A'da?"

"Just tired, sweetie."

"You've been taking care of everyone, haven't you?" Samantha said kindly. "It's high time someone took care of you, Captain. Everyone's on a break now – you have plenty of time to go get some sleep," she pointed out. "The rest of us can hold down the fort-"

"Ship," Truitt corrected her, bringing a slight smile to the young engineer's face as he imitated Konstan.

"The ship. Thanks," she finished.

Marc just looked irritated. "I haven't the time, Samantha! I've got to get us all off this planet before it kills us." He shoved his chair back and the pair leapt up. Elise appeared from behind Samantha and touched her arm.

"I'll handle it," she said lightly. She turned to Marc. "Captain, even you are subject to me when it comes to your well-being. Get some rest – doctor's orders."

"I may be subject to you," Marc replied, "but rest will have to wait. I promise, I'll get some later." Elise and Samantha exchanged a glance.

"Whatever you say," the doctor sighed, and gave Marc a one-armed hug.

"Ouch! What in the - what did you just do?" he asked quizzically. A split-second later Aiyra was catching him and lowering him into his chair.

"He'll be out for a while," Elise said cheerfully, eyeing the micro-syringe in her hand. "You wouldn't believe how many people I've had to do this to." She gave Samantha a look.

"And you'd better watch your health, too! I've lost count of how many times I've almost put you out. Aiyra is the only one on this ship who knows how to handle herself and others at the same time." Elise smiled affectionately at the girl who was cradling her father's head in her arms.

"You've been through all this before. . . there aren't many painful lessons left for you to learn."

Aiyra just kissed her father's brow. "I need to get back to the nursery," she said reluctantly. "I am supposed to be babysitting in a few minutes, but if I move, will he wake up?"

"Don't worry about him. We can wake him enough to get him to his cabin, and then he'll fall asleep again."

Elise motioned to Truitt, and together they got the captain to his feet and led him out. Samantha and Aiyra looked at each other. They understood each other quite clearly, now that they knew they shared a love for Marc and Konstan, and the trauma, gravity, and responsibility left to them by the Marauders. It was the first time they had gotten a chance to sympathize together.

"We'll be OK, won't we," Samantha whispered, drawing the girl into her arms. "Like we always told him we would be?"

"I guess so. . . but I do not feel fine anymore!"

"I know, darling, I know!"

Samantha rocked her in her arms and looked out over the crowded room and the burning sand outside. If only they could save themselves from losing anyone else!

XXV

Risk

Marc was dreaming again. A shimmering star, and a spread of open sky; the singing of a faint fountain mingled with the sweet humming of a mother to her child.

Talitha!

She came and leaned her head on his shoulder and they looked up at the sky.

Something covered the stars - Marc looked up to see the silhouette of the *Remnant* set against the sky. It remained a moment and then glided past the horizon, leaving Marc with an eerie feeling that someone was calling him from the bridge. He shook himself and looked at Talitha, who had noticed nothing.

Look, she said, *there is your star, Marc! And there is Aiyra's.* She pointed the stars out to him, and looked into the sleepy eyes of the infant she held.

Your star, she whispered. *You are the star! And your father is the sun*, she laughed, turning to look up at him, *and I will be the moon.*

Marc was laughing at her, but something was wrong – everything went cold, and a shadow reached across the stars, like a hand groping for a wandering flame –

As Marc reached out to touch his daughter's cheek, he felt that shadow touch him and freeze his blood cold, trying to draw his hand away –

Run, Talitha!

But she didn't understand, for she couldn't see.

Talitha! RUN!

And Marc was wrestling now with the shadow that blended with the night.

Marc?

And then Talitha screamed as the shadow split in two and covered her mouth and held her back, and Aiyra fell –

Ding!

Marc shot upright. No, he was only in bed, having another nightmare. How he got there was a complete blank. He blinked and saw the light flashing on the videocaller in the next room. Grabbing his coat, he got up and snapped the video on.

"Hey," he said groggily. "How long have I been asleep?"

"Long enough," Samantha smiled. "I have good news for you, Captain. The plumbing has been fixed, so we now have water. On the downside, we don't have *much* water. What little there was after the lines burst, half-evaporated in this heat."

"Great," Marc sighed. "Something tells me we won't find any water on Lythos. When does Truitt think we can get off the ground?"

"Another day or two; there's just a few parts remaining to be fixed."

Marc paused, trying to think which of the planets in the system might hold water. The answer was none of them.

"We could. . . take the *Delta's* supply, Captain."

Marc's eyes widened with surprise.

"You, of all people, would be willing to risk returning to the site?" he asked in bewilderment. "Samantha-"

"They think we're dead, Captain," she pointed out.

"Maybe so, but if they find us there again, they'll do worse than try to kill us." Marc narrowed his eyes at her. "Samantha, I can't believe you'd risk having Medhros find you. And not only that, but they'll take all of us, not just you."

"Except we have *you*," Samantha replied. "Once we get the *Lumenara* in working order, we can take one of the shuttles. Captain, there's no water anywhere else in this system – and those in the infirmary will die if we don't get it from somewhere. The Marauders are afraid of you. . . or so you told me."

"Don't use that on me, Samantha," Marc snapped.

His eyes slid to the dark sky outside the window. The massive rocks appeared as the plating on one of those ancient Earth creatures – what were they called? Stegosaurus, Marc guessed. With its bony shields and club-like tail, it could have been a dangerous weapon – only it was supposed that it was gentle.

Returning to the *Delta* might mean danger, but then again, it might mean life. The thought of the *Remnant* returned to his mind. He didn't want the *Lumenara* to become like it, an ancient forced colony that died in the inhospitable system, only to be found centuries later. But as ominous as the ship was, something nagged him.

It was as though he was being called; every time he turned his thoughts to it, the ship grew in his mind until he could think of nothing else, nor see nor hear anything but his thoughts. He saw the ship, heard the ghostly echo of thousands of voices, a sudden flash, a golden mark-

"Captain!"

Marc snapped around and saw Samantha. Her image flickered on the screen.

"Captain? Are you feeling alright?"

"I'm alright, Samantha. I need to get to the *Remnant*. When I leave for the *Delta*, I'll have a team to gather whatever is left of the water supply . . . and I'll be investigating what happened to the colonizers. Tell Truitt to get the repairs completed sooner rather than later. I want to get us all out of here."

He snapped off the video, leaving Samantha staring at her watch.

What have I gotten us into? she wondered, and hoped the answer was 'nothing.'

~~~

"Engines are up and running, sir," Topping said over his shoulder as the captain took his seat. Marc leaned forward and glanced over the glowing panels before him. The cracked screens had all been replaced and the interface repaired; all systems were functioning at 90% or above. He sat back, satisfied.

"Alright, Ensign. Let's get her off the ground!"

An outpouring of blue flame scattered the sand and bled it into pits of glass that formed beneath each of the thrusters. A mighty roar, never heard in space, shook the ship as it rose from the ground. Sand obscured the view for a moment as it swirled around the *Lumenara*, but Vidara, Briggs, and Pell were too busy cheering to notice the lack of the boring view.

"Get us out of here, Topping," Marc laughed, watching as Vidara decided to see how long she could stay on her feet as the ship rocked. Pell caught his niece as she almost fell over the computer.

The *Lumenara* shot through the atmosphere and the stars lit up again. Marc heard a cheer of relief come over the speakers on the bridge and knew that everyone felt safe again. If only he could keep them that way!

"Set a course for the dark side of Lythos," he ordered. "I want the *Lumenara* to hide there while we investigate the *Delta* and the *Remnant*; if the Marauders return, they won't be able to detect you because of the atmospheric interference."

Topping guided the ship out of the sunlight and well over the border of the shadowed half of the planet.

"Pell, get me a team for retrieving the *Delta's* water supply," Marc said, getting up. "We'll depart in one of the shuttles in thirty minutes."

The door slid open and he exited. Samantha was standing there, arms folded.

"Captain."

"Samantha." Marc eyed her, wondering what he had done now.

"I'm going with you. And I *don't* mean to the *Delta*."

"Samantha! If the Marauders are there, I would be taking you into far greater danger than leaving you on the *Lumenara*. I'm not going to run the risk of you being caught. . . You're staying right here."

Marc shook his head and walked past her on his way to the elevators. He stopped short when he realized that the engineer wasn't following him.

"Samantha?"

She was standing right where he had left her, with an amused expression. "You told me to stay right here," she laughed. "Either I go with you or I turn into a statue. Take your pick. Either way I'll be sure to annoy you."

Marc couldn't help rolling his eyes. "Well, clearly you can't stay in one spot –"

In an instant Samantha was at his side, laughing up at him and taking his arm. "So, I'm going with you. If you're being called somewhere, I should go, too. The Marauders are afraid of you, and I'll stay with you. Besides, Aiyra will stress about you being on your own."

"Mm, I never said I'd be alone," Marc replied, but Samantha had managed to dismantle all his objections in one go. "At least I can keep an eye on *you* this way."

He took her hand and pulled her along into the elevator. No one saw him take the engineer in his arms and rest her head on his heart, except for anyone who happened to be keeping an eye on the security cameras.

XXVI

Remnants

Samantha glanced out the window and watched as the *Lumenara* vanished into the deep canyons of Lythos. Marc's team were taking one of the roomy shuttles – it could easily seat a hundred passengers – around Lythos and back to its moon, Strotos, where both abandoned cruisers were caught in orbit. Samantha stood beside Marc, who was piloting. Having brought only a dozen crewmembers with them, the shuttle would easily handle taking the water supply onboard. Seven large tanks sat in the lower deck. Hopefully, there would be enough water to fill them.

A silver speck came in sight, beside a looming shadow.

"There," Marc murmured. "Let's scan for life signs. . ."

The lights flashed and the timid beep told him that the scanner found nothing. He shook his head and sighed. At least there was no way the Marauders were there. This time he made sure to double-check that there was no ship hiding anywhere near. Nothing.

"All of you, prepare to board the *Delta*. We'll dock on her starboard side. Samantha, you and I will be able to make it onto the *Remnant* from there."

He eased the shuttle up to the *Delta's* airlock and the magnetic field locked both ships in place. Marc turned and glanced at the crew.

"Ready?" They nodded. "Keep your eyes open. We don't know what the conditions are like aboard the ship – life support may be down."

The door hissed and let them into the covered walk between the shuttle and the airlock. Marc stepped up to the entry and examined the panel affixed to the wall. A strip of colored bars and sensor readings told him what he needed to know.

"Life support seems steady," he said over his shoulder. "It's not detecting any foreign material in the air: no gases, viruses, nothing."

He entered the access code and heard the locking mechanism unwind and the door slid open. Samantha cried out.

Three bodies lay sprawled on the floor. Marc and Pell dropped down to examine them. Two of them were knights, and the third was a refugee. They were dead – hence the lack of positive scans. Chemical burns riddled one, sword slashes another, and a concussion had done in the third.

"Take the bodies into the shuttle," Marc murmured to his first officer. "There may be more. . . but from the looks of this place, the Marauders rounded everyone up in here, and these three put up a fight." He glanced around.

Trash littered the floor, and the walls were scorched as though an explosive, yet non-lethal gas had been lighted to render the passengers and crew helpless. An acrid, almost incense-like scent still lingered.

"It's Martheliox," Samantha said, catching her breath as she came beside them both. "One of the engineered gases found in Borania. Sensors have a hard time detecting it because of its atomic structure."

Marc threw her a look. "You would know," he sighed. "You dealt with it. The smell does remind me of it. . . the hull plating on my ship wasn't entirely air-tight when I went through there." He stood.

The discovery of the bodies, now being transferred to the shuttle, was unsettling. Yet perhaps, in a way, not as unsettling as the discovery of two empty ships would have been. At least there was a sign of what had happened.

"Come on, everyone, let's get in and out of here as quickly as possible. Pell, take the crew down to the reservoirs on C deck. You'll have to transfer the water flow from the plumbing system to the recycling system, and then hook it up to the shuttle. Samantha, you're with me."

Marc beckoned to her and led her cautiously through the silent ship. The lights had failed, so they had to use the flashlights they had clipped to their belts. They didn't come across any other bodies, only a frightened cat that felt safe in Samantha's arms.

At last, they came to the second airlock, where the two ghost ships were locked together. This time it took several tries to find the correct code, but they finally entered the airlock. The door of the *Remnant* was rusted, and partially dented in.

"That's strange," Marc said, examining the keypad and screen beside the door. "It shows that life support is still functioning. I would have thought it would have stopped a few centuries ago – unless there were survivors here relatively recently."

"Wait! Remember, the distress signal drew us in, and it must have been the same signal which brought the *Delta* here. The Marauders may have set it off at the time, and they may have needed access to the ship in order to start it. It would make sense that they would have fixed the life support for their purposes."

"Either way, at least we know they aren't here now, and that it's relatively safe," Marc replied. He punched the 'open' button again. Nothing happened.

"And," he drawled, "we also know that the door won't open. Sheesh."

He tried a dozen codes, gave up, put his back against the doorway, slid his hand through the crack, and shoved it open. It took a few minutes and all his strength, resulting in him nearly falling flat when it finally gave way. He coughed as a cloud of dust billowed into the hallway where they were standing.

"Don't you think you want to leave that cat here?" he choked, looking at the purring gray cat on the engineer's shoulder.

"And leave her all alone to get scared again? I think not. Right, kitty?" Samantha stroked the cat's ears.

Marc just shook his head, flicked on his flashlight again, and squeezed through the doorway. Samantha followed.

There were no lights here whatsoever, and the silence, save for the soft creaking of the ancient ship, was more unsettling than anything else. Dust had fallen so thickly that their footprints were clearly marked as they crossed the lobby. A map of the ship was handily pinned to the wall.

"I don't know where I'm going," Marc muttered. "Maybe the bridge. . . the captain's quarters. But what I really want to know is what on earth happened to everyone on board?"

"The Captain's log will probably help you," Samantha replied. "Go on, Captain, I'll take the cat down to the engine room and the infirmary. I want to see what has kept this ship from crashing into Strotos all these years. . . if it was here that long."

"No, you don't, you're staying with me, like you promised you would! If the engine room and infirmary are really that important to you – wait, why the infirmary?"

"Because, if the inhabitants were killed off by someone or some*thing*, one or more cases may have been treated and taken note of in the medical log."

"Okay, that makes sense. Let's look there first."

Marc scanned the map with his watch and then led the way. They came to the heart of the *Remnant* – like the *Lumenara*, each deck gazed over those below. Though the ship was ovalesque, the core was oblong, and on the lower level was a deep reflecting pool that mirrored everything above and below.

"The engine room will be in the stern, on the lowest level," Marc whispered to his companion. "And the infirmary seems to be just two floors down."

They found the stairs and proceeded carefully – half of them were rusted through. Samantha gasped as a bolt loosened from the wall and the stairs all shook and sagged. The pair made it up in one piece and crossed the deck to the far side.

The door to the infirmary gaped open, and a few lights still glowed inside. It seemed that the solar panels on the hull still gathered enough power for these. Most of the equipment was in perfect condition, but a few pieces had been tossed about, as though a meteor had collided with the ship. Samantha got to work on one of the computers, plugging it into a portable battery she found beneath a layer of dust.

"Nothing in the log," she said softly, as Marc investigated the corners of the room. "The entries aren't even dated, so I can't tell anything from them."

Marc was trying to process this when he rounded a corner and came to a massive, tarp-covered structure. He could see pieces of shelving protruding from the loose covering, but he couldn't tell what was beneath it. The dust had been scattered, and Marc felt a chill creep up his spine as he saw a few items carelessly fallen beneath the first shelf.

"Samantha, come here."

The engineer obeyed, and stopped short.

"What is – why do I get the feeling I don't want to know?" she breathed.

"Only one way to find out," Marc answered tersely.

Taking a deep breath, he seized the edge of the tarp and pulled it away. The shelves contained the bodies of the crewmembers and passengers, men, women, and children, who looked more to be asleep than dead. Samantha held a medical scanner over them. Not even the faintest life signs were present, which could, indeed, have escaped the shuttle's scanners.

"Captain, that's not all," Samantha gasped, staring at the screen. "These people died only thirty years ago!" She glanced at him and he saw how pale she was.

"*Only?*" Marc whispered. "Samantha, they look like they died yesterday."

"The scanner is picking up traces of CO_2 and natronian gases in their lungs," she said softly. "I don't know how the latter came to be on the ship – possibly some foreign material they brought on board.

It's a preserving agent used in some cultures for embalming bodies without too much effort. It does not appear that this was done on purpose on the *Remnant*, but that it leaked into the air and preserved the bodies for the past thirty years."

"At least we know that neither of those gases are present now since our scanners didn't pick up anything," Marc muttered, feeling sick.

He replaced the tarp, knowing that these bodies would not be able to be taken back to the *Lumenara* for burial. There were just too many. . . there must have been at least five hundred.

"What I want to know is, who placed the bodies here?" he asked. "Did some survive for thirty years before being captured by the Marauders? If so, they may have set off the distress signal. But there's no way they could have survived here for so long – how did this ship manage for two centuries without contacting anyone?"

"All I know, sir, is that the Marauders do have a respect for the dead. . . if they came aboard the *Remnant*, as we suppose, they likely would have done this for them."

"But why not with the three on the *Delta*? It doesn't add up."

"It seems to me that the ship that attacked us was piloted by Marauder mercenaries," Samantha murmured. "They don't share all of the Marauders' ideas; in fact, they are much worse. I would not expect them to treat the dead with care; and I would not expect the Marauders to kill three men even if they put up a fight, if they could be enslaved instead."

Marc exhaled and looked around. Samantha's new pet was walking on a high shelf above the medicine cabinets; the engineer stretched out her arms, calling softly to it, and it bounced from the shelf to Marc's shoulder and then into her arms.

"Oof, that's a heavy cat! You like them, don't you?" Marc asked, rubbing his shoulder.

"I grew up with several. And a big dog. You don't like cats, do you," she teased.

"No, not really. Aside from the fact that Aiyra has one. I figured it would be less rambunctious than a dog. What kind of dog was yours?"

"Gelert was a Almedran hound. Even when he was a baby, he was huge. He was only a year old when I lost him, and his head was up to my waist. I don't know how big he would be now."

"Wait, what happened to him?" Marc asked.

"I don't know," the engineer replied, stepping out. "He disappeared when Medrhos left my planet. He liked the dog," she shrugged. "I wouldn't be surprised if he took Gelert with him."

Marc followed her.

"I want to head to the bridge," he said softly. "Let me check on Pell first." He called his first officer and found that the process of transferring the water supply was nearly complete. Marc snapped off the video.

"We'll have to move fast," he told Samantha. "They should be ready to go in about fifteen minutes. The bridge is on the tenth level, just opposite where we came in."

He took the stairs two at a time, but Samantha was more cautious in following. After all, it is a bit harder to see when your arms are full of a twelve-pound, purring cat. The captain was so intent on reaching his destination while keeping track of the time, that he neglected to remember this fact. When Samantha reached the top of the stairs, she found that he was nowhere in sight. Moreover, the cat decided that it would be a good time to jump down and stretch.

"Kitty!" Samantha exclaimed.

The stairs behind her suddenly fell a foot lower with a resounding crash. The cat jumped and ran down a different corridor than the one Marc had taken. The engineer groaned. She wasn't about to leave the poor cat on its own, not now that she was fond of it. Samantha glanced over her shoulder and shrugged. The ship was empty anyway, and Marc would be able to call her easily enough. She went down the corridor and vanished as though into the shadowy jaws of Cerberus.

XXVII

Memoir

Marc slipped into the cobwebbed bridge. No lights, no hum of machinery, and no sign that anyone had been there recently - except for the handprint beside the emergency signal. He went through the Captain's desk and that of the first officer, but found nothing that told of the disaster, unless one counted the spiders that clung to his hands when he reached inside.

Marc shook them off and carefully navigated the pitch-black room. If he recalled correctly, the captain's quarters were just off the left of the bridge. He found the handle and slid it open with a soft squeaking sound. Everything seemed to still be in perfect order, as though the captain had only left it that morning.

He searched the desk and the drawers until he came across an old data log tucked under the mattress of the alcove bed. He plugged it into the multi-purpose battery on his flashlight and the screen flashed on. There were thousands of entries spread over those five hundred years. Marc muttered under his breath and tried to find something that would tell him what happened on the ship. He finally found it, under a log started by Captain Jen Aoslin in 1820.

The ship had been searching for a colonizing system – the passengers could never quite agree on a place, and every time they tried to set up a colony, something would happen to set them back. Fires, strange creatures, floods, suppressive heat. . . .

So, the years passed, with a summer spent on one planet, winter on another, until they had learned how to survive in every environment, even those most hostile.

Marc's eyes widened as he read. The ship had encountered a massive, destructive asteroid field, where every collision sparked an explosion of the gases contained within each boulder. The *Remnant* had been forced to bombard the field with its lasers in order to clear a safe path –

The lasers caused a chain reaction within the field, the captain had written. *Soon every boulder was exploding, big and small. . . and we were left sitting in a cloud of swirling pink gases, as though a thousand whirlpools were stirring there. Without warning, we were drawn into one and were instantly someplace else – and not only someplace else, but some* time *else. We had gone back almost a thousand years – the Mândrauers, a newborn slave trade empire, were struggling to control the falling worlds.*

Marc turned to the next captain's log.

For years, it was not hard to escape them, until they discovered our entrance to their time and began to utilize it for their own ends. They soon controlled the portals as one learns to control a wild horse, and we could scarcely outrun them. They came to be known as the Marauders. On September 29th, 2435 A.D. our time, and 1384 A.D. in the time we had been in, we were finally tracked down by the Mândrauers and attacked. The Remnant *sustained heavy damage, but we finally managed to escape and the portals brought us to our own time.*

Here the Captain's narrative ended, and the computer filled in.

The damage done to the Remnant *by the mercenaries' firepower opened cracks in the hull and wreaked havoc on life support. CO_2 flooded the cabins, and natronian gas had swept through the ship when it took the portal. The captain scarcely had time to get a quarter of the colonizers off the ship in the escape pods, many of which had been too greatly damaged to offer any safety.*

Marc heard again what he had told his daughter –

"*I don't know where I'm from, Aiyra. I was born on a space freighter in unclaimed territory, with no ties to anywhere; and my parents were of a long line of colonists who – well, never colonized. Eventually their country was forgotten.*"

His heart raced as he looked again at the long list of captains, and the last. The computer had coded most of them, but he opened the file and found there the name of Jack Hesslin. Could it only be a coincidence that it was his father's name? His mother, Zendira, had often told him how his father had died saving their lives when Marc was only three years old – that the freighter had gone down. He dropped the log and shoved open the door to the adjoining room.

The lace curtains, lilac blossoms on the bedspread, and the familiar organza scarf with its floral print told him that it had, indeed, been his mother's room. The blood seemed to drain from Marc's head, leaving him dizzy as he tried to understand it all. His eyes swept the room desperately, looking for something that could help him. Something gold glinted on the wall, dangling from the edge of a damaged jewelry case. Marc freed it and rubbed the medallion free of dust. It was the size of his palm, and in the lattice-like pattern were embraced a tiny star and moon, and between them a voyaging ship, bound to the background of a cross.

Again!

His father paused in the act of replacing the medallion around his neck and laughed, tossing it in the air for his son to catch in the arms of his mother.

Why not? It will belong to you one day; you'll wear it when the ship is yours.

Smiling, Jack slipped the cord over his head as a sound like thunder crashed and the ship shook. A dizzying blur, the thunderstorm – or was it? – a furious flash of wine and rose, and everything went silent.

Zendira, take the child and go! He heard his father say. *Before the ship breaks up inside. Gas is flooding the ship and she won't hold – Go! Goodbye, my little ones.* He kissed them both and the door of the escape shuttle slammed shut.

Marc's eyes flew open. He was clutching the medallion so tightly that it was cutting into his fingers. Everything was coming to a full circle. A sharp beep pierced the heavy air of his mother's chamber and Marc ducked back into the other room. The sound had pierced something else: Marc had been so intent on his work that he had forgotten Samantha.

Where was she?! Why hadn't she stayed at his side as she had promised? His heart began to race as he realized that the beeping was coming from an eerily lit scanner that had just flickered to life. It took him just a split-second to realize that there were too many life signs on the *Remnant* – much more than one engineer and a cat.

XXVIII

Judgment

"Pell!" Marc said tersely, snapping on his watch. "Where are you?"

"Just loading the last of the water supply. Are you ready?" the first officer replied, hearing the stress in his captain's voice.

"No, I'm not ready," Marc growled. "Get the crew out of here, Pell, and make for the *Lumenara* as fast as you can! And don't ask questions!"

He slammed his hand on the desk and called Samantha. He watched her icon flicker on the screen as the other life signs drew nearer to it. She still had a few minutes, but that wasn't enough.

"Samantha!"

At that moment, Samantha was crouched in one of the cabins, trying to persuade the cat to come out from under the bed, when she heard Marc's voice.

"Captain – what is it?"

"We aren't alone. I don't know who or what is on this ship, but you'll be surrounded within two minutes. I need you to get back to the entrance to the *Delta*! I'll meet you there."

"I'm on my way!" Samantha dropped everything, shoved herself under the bed, snatched the cat, and stuffed her into a backpack she had found. "Don't worry, I'm not leaving you out here," she muttered, and ran.

Doors, doors, and more doors flashed by. Her heart raced as her ears picked up faint sounds behind her. The cat squeaked in distress as it bounced with every stride Samantha made - the feline's glowing eyes saw the distant shadows that the engineer did not, and hastily tucked itself into a ball, hoping that Samantha would keep her safe.

There, ahead lay the heart of the ship! Without slowing her pace, Samantha vaulted over the handrail, landing on her feet on the smoothed edge of the first set of stairs, and slid down as swiftly as they could carry her. She leapt onto the second staircase, heart pounding in her ears. Marc couldn't be far now – the door to the *Delta* was only a few yards from the bottom of the stairs. She ran down them but no sooner had she landed on the middle step when the bolts ripped from the wall!

The cat screeched as Samantha tumbled from the falling stairs. There was nothing to grab but thin air. She fell eighty feet to the floor below. The last thing she saw was a huge shadow bounding towards her as everything went black.

~~~

Marc? Marc! Samantha tried to cry out as she wandered a maze of darkness. He had to be close by; he hadn't been far when she had fallen. Then she realized she was dreaming and woke up. Everything was suddenly bright, as though all the lights in the ship had been turned on at once. She had only been out for a few moments. She closed her eyes, half-blinded.

If she hadn't slowed her fall by pushing off and away from the stairs falling with her, and if Almedrans weren't skilled in free-falling without dying, she would have been killed. Every Almedran learned the skill, for the best silk was found high in the mountains where the gentle Almedran spiders dwelt. The only way back down from those near-vertical peaks was via waterfall or a series of free-falls. Samantha had managed to land on her feet and roll, but the impact caused her to black out.

Samantha felt a touch on her hand and opened her eyes again. She still couldn't see, but the cat was licking her fingers. She shook her head to clear her vision and realized that it wasn't the cat. The cat was still huddled in her backpack a few feet away, terrified. Instead, it was a giant dog that was crouching over her! His happy, lopsided smile and particolored green and purple eyes were familiar.

"Gelert!" Samantha gasped, and her hands went to her head. Could she be imagining it? But she sank her hands into the fur of his neck as she had done when he was a baby, and he woofed happily and danced around her, nudging her to try and get her to her feet. He was almost four and a half feet tall at the head now, Samantha supposed.

"Good boy!" she breathed. "We need to go!" She sat up and then realized they had run out of time.

"I've been waiting for you." A black-gloved hand was extended to her and a chill ran through her.

Medrhos!

~~~

Tiger eyes and hair shaded like the deepest topaz, ebony and scarlet, and a dozen armed men. Medrhos pulled her to her feet.

"It's a shame you had to fall so that I could catch you – just not unfortunately in a manner that would avoid injury. This ship is falling apart after five hundred years. I'm glad neither of us forgot our training on Almedra."

He gently brushed a lock of hair out of her face and inspected the rapidly darkening bruise on her temple. Samantha caught her breath and jerked her hand free. She was afraid; this was, of course, not the Medrhos that she knew, but the one who was ruthless, unpredictable, and kept all at an arm's length. But she couldn't let him know that she was afraid.

"If you think I'm happy to see you, I'm not," she said flatly, taking a step back.

Gelert pushed his nose into her side and she dropped her hand on his head. Medrhos cocked his head with a patronizing smile.

"You haven't changed, Samantha. Not in the way I would have wished. Yet you still think you can take care of yourself. . . last time you nearly fell from the mountain river thinking you could save yourself, and see who has to look after you both times?"

"I hardly think this case counts as one of 'you looking after me," Samantha said scornfully. "But I won't take that bait, Medrhos. Why have you betrayed me, twice? Friends don't easily become enemies except when a lie is thrown in from the start."

"And that," Medrhos laughed, "I could translate as, 'why did you take my dog from me?' For if I don't wish to answer the full question, I can answer part of it. Quite simply, he's a good dog, and since I couldn't bring you with me, I brought your dog instead."

Gelert whined softly and licked Medrhos' glove.

"Good boy!" the Marauder king said affectionately, tugging the dog's ears. "As far as lying goes. . . " his eyes glinted. "You will learn not to accuse me of possessing a forked tongue, Samantha. But come. Now that you are with me again, you will stay with me, just as Gelert has."

He extended his hand once more to the girl who stood glaring at him.

"Come, princess. . . it's time to go."

"You're right, it *is* time for *you* to go," Samantha replied, snapping her fingers. Gelert bounded to her side in an instant. "I'll be watching you from the bridge."

"Nice try," Medrhos smirked. "You can't escape, and I don't give up easily. Unfortunately for you, my dear, I already thought of this years ago." He grabbed her shoulder and lightly laid his hand against her brow. The scar burned so hot that Samantha cried out and collapsed into his arms.

"I didn't want to do that to you, nor to have to bring you back as my prisoner," the king said softly. "It would have been better if you had taken my hand. Coran!" he called over his shoulder. A man dressed all in sable leather and plating stepped forward. "Get ready to leave. The *Delta* and the *Remnant* can keep on drifting."

"For the sake of the friendship we had," Samantha moaned, "please – don't – Medrhos!"

The king froze for a moment, looking at the girl who was now supported by Coran. Medrhos' eyes flickered a moment as though a shield were falling. He steeled himself.

"You'll feel better about it when we get underway. Take her to the ship," he ordered.

"You aren't taking her anywhere!"

Medrhos whirled around and Samantha shook herself awake. Marc stood on the balustrade high above them, his father's medallion gleaming around his neck and his plasma blade blazing. He leapt from the railing.

"You took my wife from me," he said, his voice dangerously low. "The nobleman you sold her to, killed her. I won't let you take Samantha! How I've longed to stand here and challenge you for what you've done to them both."

"And I've longed to meet you as well," Medrhos returned, his half-open eyes watching Marc like a crouching tiger. "I've wanted to show my men that you're no one to be afraid of!"

Neither man moved, and Medrhos' men stood silently behind them as Marc's blade sputtered viciously.

"Do you realize that you nearly killed her as well?" he asked the king, breaking the silence. "You nearly destroyed thousands of lives when you opened fire on us, including the one you seem to think most precious."

"My mercenaries took too much freedom with their orders," Medrhos said warily. "I never destroy a ship except in battle. I don't care about your precious *Lumenara* now – I have the only one I ever wanted, and I couldn't care less whether the rest escape."

He contemplated having Gelert leap on the captain, but the dog was too fascinated by the newcomer to be of service.

"And as for not allowing me to 'get away with this,' how do you think you're going to accomplish that?" Medrhos inquired, turning back to Marc. "I have Samantha, and you don't. I don't even need a weapon."

He stared when Marc laughed and threw aside his blade. It fell with a clatter and rolled under the fallen stairs.

"Neither do I! You may think you have all the cards, O 'king', and your plans *will* work as you desire; but in the end they will all fail for one card you don't possess."

Bewildered, Medrhos signaled to his men and they grabbed Marc's arms and threw him on the floor. He didn't struggle.

"Do you think, Hesslin, that I don't know of your family history? I drew the *Delta* here so that you would follow and regain the knowledge of your family legacy. Your ancestors opened the time warp field and gave us the chance to tame it and take it for our own; and oh, how the slave trade grew once we knew we could make a raid at any point in time!"

Marc paled slightly. "You know as well as I do, Medrhos, that one cannot be responsible for what was done by others when one did not even exist, and not even your people knew what would happen because of the fields."

"A good point, I will admit," Medrhos murmured, pacing slowly as he eyed the captain. "I hope you also realize that you must face the consequences of trying to undo your past; I've been told your kind embrace history and remember it, and that changing it is considered an evil. Unlike your ancestors, you are no friend to the Marauders," he sighed, shaking his head as though in disappointment.

"If your ancestors considered my father their friend, I'm not sure I care to know what you do to your enemies," Marc said sarcastically, casting his eyes over the evidence of the *Remnant's* last fight.

Medrhos snorted and kicked Marc's blade up into his own hand. He flicked it on. "I suppose this is 'futuristic,'" he remarked. "Yet I've seen better technology on my side of the fields."

He measured the blade and a steel beam with his eyes and then struck out, cleaving the metal shaft in two with a furious shower of sparks. He leapt backwards as the beam crashed to the floor.

"-But it gets the job done," he observed. He turned to Marc, the blade still in hand, his intentions obvious.

"Medrhos, no!" Samantha gasped.

She wrested her arms free from Coran's grip and held the Marauder king back. Medrhos caught his breath and stopped himself mid-swing. He threw a sideways glance at Samantha and she realized that he had wanted her to stop him. Her heart sank and she knew she had only one choice.

"Don't kill him," she faltered. "I'll go with you if you promise not to hurt him, or anyone else that I love." She bit her lip and wished she had caught her tongue a few seconds before. A half-angry yet pleased look flashed over her captor's face.

"Then pass judgment!" he replied, powering down the blade. "And be swift, Samantha."

She stared into Marc's eyes, but he only smiled and nodded ever so slightly. She took a deep breath and whispered into Medrhos' ear.

"As you wish!" He flung aside Marc's blade and drew a strange pistol from the holster on his right arm. The fiery bubble it created exploded with a hiss, but it wasn't aimed at Marc – Samantha gasped. It was a vortex not unlike one of the time warps in Borania. They didn't even need to travel that far! So, this was how hundreds aboard the *Delta* could vanish in an instant - had her plan already failed?

"You have been judged!" Medros proclaimed. "And you are fortunate to retain your life, Hesslin. . . . if you're lucky, you just may find your wife waiting for you. Try not to lose her again; there's only time enough for one wedding here!" he mocked. "Throw him in!"

His eyes glowed and his face flushed with unusual pleasure at such an easy victory.

"Marc!" Samantha cried, leaping forward as the captain was dragged to his feet.

"Samantha!" He was still smiling, and Samantha momentarily forgot their predicament as she gazed up into his face. He wasn't afraid for either of them, and he wasn't afraid of Medrhos; and he had finally realized that even God did not place the blame on him for Talitha's death, Aiyra's lost childhood, or Samantha's capture.

"Oh, Marc! I love you," Samantha whispered, suddenly so proud of him that she was blinded by a few tears. Her captain's eyes lit up and he grinned at her.

"You said it first. Don't worry about me, Samantha."

Medrhos was staring, silhouetted by the flashing light of the vortex. "Throw him in!" he shouted again over its deepening roar, snatching Samantha's arm and jerking her back.

But Marc didn't need to be moved. Eyes fastened on the pair, he stepped backwards with an insolent smile and was sucked into the portal's beating heart.